STORIES OF
SURVIVAL

Australian Speculative Fiction

Edited by Austin P. Sheehan,
Lisa Rodrigues & S. M. Isaac

First published by Deadset Press in 2021.

Cover design Copyright © Pamela Jeffs.

Edited by Austin P. Sheehan, Lisa Rodrigues and S. M. Isaac.

ISBN: 978-0-6450228-2-7

Supporting

Melanoma
Institute Australia

Acknowledgements.

In the spirit of reconciliation, Deadset Press acknowledges the Traditional Custodians of country throughout Australia and their connections to land, sea and community. We pay our respect to their Elders past and present and extend that respect to all Aboriginal and Torres Strait Islander peoples today.

This charity anthology has been put together to honour the legacy of Aiki Flinthart, who lost her battle with cancer in early 2021, and to all those in our lives who have battled or are battling cancer. Accordingly, all proceeds will be donated to the Melanoma Institute of Australia.

We must also thank the members of the Australian Speculative Fiction community who gave so much of their time helping put this collection together, especially Pamela Jeffs, S. M. Isaac, Lisa Rodrigues, Maureen Flynn, Alice Lam, Sue-Ellen Pashley, Eleanor Whitworth, Claire Fitzpatrick, Heather Ewings, Leanbh Pearson and Alanah Andrews.

— Austin P. Sheehan, on behalf of Deadset Press.

Dedication.

Survival is for the strong, or so it's said. For those souls brave enough to face down the trials thrown at them by circumstance and fate. But I believe otherwise. Survival surpasses any physical act of defiance. It can be about memory – about inspiration and the giving of hope to others who cannot rise above their own trials. It is about grit, about spirit and transcendence.

Stories of Survival is a collection presented by Deadset Press and written to honour a brilliant author and my close personal friend Aiki Flinthart. At the time of my writing this, she faces an insurmountable battle. There is no win for the war she fights. But we can see to it that she survives. She is brave and kind. Her messages and philosophies on life live on in the stories she has gifted the world and in the lessons she has crafted for the writers who will follow her. Her legacy is strong and it tells a story of survival.

So I invite you to open the pages of the following collection. Join us in honouring and celebrating the incredible woman who is Aiki Flinthart.

– Pamela Jeffs.

Contents:

The Storyteller

Kylie Fennell

In honour of all those who have faced the enemy that is cancer. For those still fighting, those who lived to tell the tale, and those no longer with us. May we remember and share your stories of courage and lives well lived.

#

There was a time when they would listen to my stories. That time is gone. They are gone. Others came in their place but they don't see me. I feel older than time itself yet I am beyond notice. My voice goes unheard. My words lost in the wind. My memories swallowed up by the earth. I cannot live forever but the stories must live on. It is up to me to ensure they survive, but I have failed—I have failed to find the Storyteller. Now the only hope is that they will find me.

* * *

The animal's screams pierce the air, awakening something deep inside the boy—a primal instinct to do something. The creature is crying for help.

He runs across the paddock to the stockyard, kicking up clouds of dust in his wake. The massive grey stallion is tethered to a timber fence railing, hooves stamping the ground, nostrils flared.

From the safety of the other side of the fence, the boy's stepbrothers cackle, striking the horse with a branch as thick as their arms. The twins, entranced by their torturous game, don't notice his approach.

The horse struggles against the rope, trying to get away. The twine has etched a bloody ring around its neck. Angry red welts arc its belly.

The boy flings open the gate to the yard so hard that it rebounds off the fence, jolting the twins to attention.

"Get out of there," yells one of the twins.

"Or we'll tell our father," says the other one.

Ignoring the threats, the boy takes a deep breath and approaches the stallion slowly. He makes placating hand gestures and shushing sounds. "I heard you."

The stallion rears and the boy stumbles back to avoid its plate-sized hooves. He tries to approach the horse again, even slower this time. "I'm not going to let anything happen to you."

The horse snorts, bulging eyes searching for its torturers.

"Don't worry about them . . ." the boy takes a small step forward, ". . . I'm here . . ." another step forward. ". . . I'm going to take care of you . . ." He is close enough to grasp the rope.

He doesn't know how or why, but he is certain the horse understands him. "I'm just going to untie this rope."

"No ya not!" one twin says.

"We're gettin' Father," says the other and they run in the direction of the main work shed.

The boy's heart quickens. His stepfather is a terrifying prospect, but he has to help the animal. "Listen," he whispers. "We don't have much time. I'm going to let you go and you need to run. Run as fast as you can. Get out of here and don't come back. Do you hear me?"

The horse's breathing slows and it nods. It understands.

The boy fumbles trying to untie the rope as running footsteps pound the dry ground. The heavy fall of his stepfather's boots is instantly recognisable. He takes his dad's pocketknife from his shorts pocket and cuts the rope.

The horse snorts in acknowledgement before galloping from the yard. The stepfather stumbles to avoid the animal as it thunders past. He splutters through the swirling dust.

Regaining his footing he advances on the boy, holding his belt aloft. "Boy!"

He rarely uses the boy's actual name. When he does, he curls his lips up in disgust, demanding to know: *"What kind of man would call his son that?"*

3

The boy staggers backwards until he is pressed against the fence. There's no escape. If his mother were home, she might do something, but with the drought, she has to work two jobs in town.

The leather hisses through the air before biting into the boy's bare legs. He grits his teeth, refusing to give his stepfather the satisfaction of hearing him scream. He ignores the twins' gleeful cries as their father strikes him again and again.

Eventually, his stepfather yields. Sweat drips down his face, he pants, "What 'ave ya . . . got to say . . . for y'self?"

The boy says nothing.

His stepfather shakes his head. "Y're a bloody disgrace. That brumby was our best chance of makin' any money this month. I had a buyer lined up and everythin'."

The boy stays silent, infuriating his stepfather further.

The man casts him a hate-filled gaze.

"Y're a waste of space, boy. Just an extra bloody mouth to feed."

"You tell 'im," the twins crow in unison.

"Go and find that stallion, *boy.*" He leans in close, the smell of tobacco and stale grog smacks the boy in the face. "And don't bother comin' back without it. Not even ya mother can save ya if you don't bring that beast back."

The boy believes him.

Trying to banish the image of the smirking twins and his self-righteous stepfather from his mind, the boy heads in the direction the horse ran. He had no idea whether he'd be coming back.

* * *

Hooves reverberate through the earth, heralding the arrival of the grey one. Lathered in sweat he stops beside me to catch his breath. He must have escaped. I'm glad for it. He's not made for domestication. They would never have tamed him, only broken him.

"Don't stay too long," I say, as he walks down to the bank to take water from the river that is a dribbling remnant of its former self. "They'll be coming for you."

The grey one snorts in response. The red welts that criss-cross his flank and belly don't escape my notice.

"Go back to the hills. To your herd. You'll be safe there."

But the stallion is tired. He lies down and rests until the sun is low on the horizon.

I'm nervous for him. But what else can I do? I have warned him.

Then a crackle of leaves and twigs underfoot tells me a small one approaches. Not the hard-faced man whose words are as vicious as his fists. One of the identical ones? *Please no.* I hope for the grey one that it's the other boy.

And it is.

Recognising his bony frame and hollow eyes, devoid of life but lacking the others' cruelty, I relax.

Some days this one comes down to the river, face wet with tears. With skin red and raw, he cries on the riverbank and talks to himself and a lost father. He's not like the other boys who take pleasure in ripping the wings off insects . . . but he is still one of them.

The stallion is back on its feet. His back is to the river but he could still evade the boy.

"Grey one, you must go."

"Hey there." The boy approaches the horse slowly, carefully.

The grey one doesn't move.

"You can't trust him, he'll take you back there."

My words are wasted on the horse but the boy looks at me, furrowing his brow in concentration before shaking his head. He returns his attention to the grey one. "C'mon, boy. Please just come back with me," he begs. "I'll protect you."

The grey one appears frozen to the ground like he's entranced by the boy.

"Get out of here while you still can."

The boy's head swivels in my direction. "Who said that?" He pulls out a pocketknife and waves it in the air with shaking hands. "Come out and face me."

Surely he can't hear me. "I'm right here," I say, testing him.

The boy's jaw drops and he stares right at me. "It's you . . . ? You're the one talking . . . ?"

"Who else would it be?"

The boy shakes his head again. "It must be the heat playing tricks on me."

At that moment the grey one gallops away.

"No, no, no," the boy sobs in the fading light. "I can't go back there without the horse . . . he'll kill me. What am I going to do?"

"You can stay here," I suggest.

He looks straight at me and scratches his head. "I understand the grey stallion . . ." He's speaking to himself. ". . . I s'pose it's not too different . . ."

"I'm not a horse."

"No. You're a gum tree . . . a *talking* gum tree," he says, waving his hands around. "You can't be real."

"But I am real. It's just that most people can't hear me . . . Actually, no-one has heard me for . . . I can't remember how long . . ."

"It can't be real. It can't be real," he chants over and over.

"Tell me. Do you have a name?"

The boy stops chanting and kicks the ground with his bare feet. "It's Neptune."

"Your name's Neptune?"

"I know, it's a stupid—"

7

"Something tells me there is a story behind that name."

The boy's eyes spark to life. "Well . . . there is. Do you want to hear it?"

"Of course. I am a Story Tree after all." The boy arches a curious brow. "Please . . . Go on . . . with your story."

"You see . . . my dad was a fisherman. He loved the sea. So did my mother. She used to help him on his fishing boat. They were out at sea when Mum went into early labour—I was born right there on the boat."

"You were born at sea?"

"Yes. That's how I got the name. Neptune is the Roman god of the sea. He's also the controller of winds, storms and—" Realisation dawns over the boy's face.

"—and horses," I finish for him.

"Right . . . horses."

"Where's your father now?"

The light vanishes from the boy's eyes. "He died. In a storm at sea."

"I'm sorry to hear that." There's an awkward pause. "So . . . How did you come to be here?"

"After Dad died, Mum got a job at the local hotel. My stepfather, whose wife had died, promised to take care of me and Mum—he probably just wanted someone to look after his kids and to cook and clean for him. Anyway, he was real nice to her, back then. So Mum agreed to marry him . . ." his voice turned bitter, ". . . just to end up *here*."

"It's a long way from the sea."

"You know, I reckon that's one of the reasons Mum married him. As much as she loved it there, I think she wanted to get as far away from the coast as possible. She never forgave the sea for taking Dad from her . . ." The boy's voice trails away in a sigh.

"Neptune—that is a fine name—thank you for sharing your story with me."

The boy nods. "It's getting dark. I've gotta get back."

"But I need to tell you my stories." The words tumble from me. I have so much I need to tell him.

"I'll be back soon . . ." a shadow crosses his face. ". . . As soon as I can."

* * *

When Neptune comes back a week or so later, we don't talk about the yellow bruise that rings his eye or how his arm is in a sling.

"So what does a Story Tree do?" he asks.

"I am the keeper of this Country's stories. It is my job to ensure those stories survive, to pass them on to those who can be trusted to safeguard them."

"Like who?"

"You, Neptune. The fact you can hear me means you are worthy . . . You will be my storyteller."

The boy looks down and rubs the back of his neck. I can tell he is not used to anyone saying he is worthy of anything, but there is a hint of a smile on his face.

"So, are you ready?"

"Ready?"

"To hear my stories."

"Yes please." He nods vigorously. "Where will you start?"

"At the very beginning of course. Before your time, before mine. Before there was anything . . ."

* * *

Neptune treasures his time with the Story Tree. He visits most days, getting up before dawn, so he can finish his jobs early and get to the riverbank. No-one notices or cares where he goes—even his step-father ignores him following the 'punishment' and the resulting argument with Neptune's mother, as long as his work is done. And with each day that passes, the Country around the boy comes to life. Every sense tingles. He can hear the tiniest of sounds from the smallest of creatures. He's becoming in tune with every living thing.

This particular day, Neptune is heading towards the riverbank when a sound stops him in his tracks. From the bushland bordering the home paddock comes the sound of the twins laughing. Coming from the same direction is a high-pitched squealing—something in pain.

Neptune finds the twins squatting over an ant nest. One of them holds a magnifying glass and directs a beam of sizzling light onto a line of ants scurrying in and out of the nest.

"Stop it!" Neptune shouts.

The twins scowl up at him. "Get lost," one says, and the other goes back to burning the ants.

"I said stop it!"

The twin who told Neptune to go stands up and crosses his arms. "Make us!"

"Yeah, what are you going to do about it?" the other demands, his eyes leaving the magnifying glass.

As one twin shoves Neptune, the other twin eggs his brother on to push Neptune harder, oblivious to what's going on at his feet.

While the twins focus on Neptune, the light from the magnifying glass catches on a pile of leaves. In a matter of seconds, flames are leaping across the ground.

"Look what you've done," one twin squeals.

"Dad's going to kill you," the other says and they run off to find their father.

Panic ripples through Neptune's body. A strong wind fans the growing fire, its flames nearly as tall as him. It looks like it's heading away from the house, straight towards the river . . . towards the Story Tree.

As Neptune sprints through the bush, he prays that his stepfather can put the fire out. *He'll call the rural fire service. They'll stop it.* He prays that the wind dies down, or changes direction. But his prayers go unheard.

The fire is at Neptune's heels when he reaches the riverbank. Towering flames lick the sky.

Neptune slumps down under the Story Tree and cries for the fate of his friend.

"It's all right. I've survived worse," the tree says.

It's hard to imagine anything worse than the wall of fire before them. It's like nothing Neptune has seen before. A life force of its own. A hungry beast, devouring the land, consuming everything in its path.

The heat is unbearable. Visibility: Zero. Neptune chokes on the acrid smoke as the fire howls towards them. Nothing will survive it.

"Neptune, get in the water. Go to the other side of the river."

"But you . . . your stories. You haven't told me all of them yet."

"All you need to do, Neptune, is listen. Listen to the earth, the air, the water. Listen to this Country and you will hear the stories. Now go!"

THE STORYTELLER

* * *

I'm not sure how long I'm in the darkness. I don't remember much, but I do remember the excruciating pain as the flames overtook my limbs. So different to the slow-burning, scorching sensation of fires past. I'm incinerated in a screaming fiery whoosh. My stories vapourised with me.

After what might have been days or weeks – years even, the light appears again.

Something is different though. I don't feel the weight of my body. I feel lighter. I *am* lighter. I'm a shadow of myself. I am a small green shoot pushing through the blackened earth. I am not whole. Something other than my centuries-old branches is missing.

The next day a smiling boy greets me.

"It's you. You survived! I mean, I did my research . . ." the boy rambles. "I read that eucalypt mallee trees can shoot again from their lignotuber—the 'mallee root'," his voice rises in excitement, "and I'd hoped but—"

"Who are you?"

The boy's face crumples. "It's me. Neptune."

Images. Words. Memories. All of it comes flooding back to me. "You're the Storyteller."

"Yes, I am." His grin threatens to split his face. "And you . . . you are the Story Tree."

About the Author:

Kylie Fennell is an Australian speculative fiction author of European and Aboriginal descent (Bundjalung and Gumbaynggirr). She lives in Brisbane (Yuggera Country) and has made a 25-year career out of wrangling words. If she wasn't a writer, she'd be a superhero librarian – conquering the Dewey Decimal System by day and saving the world one book at a time by night. Her short stories have appeared in several anthologies and she has published a YA fantasy series – The Kyprian Prophecy. *You can find out more at* www.kyliefennell.com.

The Forgotten Sea

Louise Zedda-Sampson

I dedicate this story to Aiki and Claire, both touched in such terrible ways by the horrible C. Sometimes words are not enough.

\#

The clock on the dash says three-o-five pm. I'm on time; Rob's late. I start work and make some notes. *Red brick, double-fronted, no fence.* I've been to hundreds of places like this: family homes neglected once the children have fled. *Welcoming . . . elusive?* I cross elusive out. Four long windows face the street, blinds half closed like lazy eyelids. The driveway widens as it meets the road: yawning, open, inviting.

"I'm waiting for Rob," I tell the house, then wonder why, tapping my pen. It's just a house. *Set in a quiet pocket, this family home will offer —*

The knock on the window makes me jump. I press hard on the steering wheel and my neck pops as I whip around. It takes a second or two to work out the blaring noise is my car horn.

Rob stands next to the car, laughing. I shoot him a dirty look and a half smile. "Yeah, good one, Rob."

"C'mon then," he says, opening my car door. "Let's go inside. Pretty ordinary, eh?" he doesn't wait for an answer. "How's it going?"

We fall into easy banter about unimportant things. He's older and treats me as a daughter. Or maybe it's more like I treat him as a father.

The sun disappears behind a cloud as we walk up the driveway. A chill wind rises. Autumn leaves scurry around my feet and I rub my arms, failing to suppress a shiver. I don't know when I stopped, but Rob's already up the steps.

"What are you doing?" Rob says.

I offer a weak smile and return to my notes. *Carport to covered entranceway, where '70s charm awaits.* A black-and-white rectangular doorbell is mounted on the door frame and the solid-oak door has a metal knocker. The memory claws at something deep inside as I climb the three stone steps. My sister peers through amber panels to the left, face pressed hard against the glass. A shadow moves behind the peephole. I blink and it's all gone. No doorbell. No solid oak. No peephole. And no sister.

"It's vacant. We did the photos earlier," Rob says. He tries several keys in the lock. None of them work. He curses under his breath, mumbles something about them maybe being the wrong keys.

"This one!" he says as the lock yields and the door creeps open. The steady tick of a clock is close but also far away, like an echo. Rob's still hunched at the lock as the door gapes wide.

He looks at me and straightens. "Guess we go inside," he says. "Maybe it's not vacant after all." He says this as a joke, but it's not funny. I already want to turn around and leave.

Ugly and large paisley leaves, amber and white, run in parallel lines on walls. A gold eight-pointed star with a round clock in the centre sits high near the ceiling, keeping a time all of its own.

A sea of lime-green carpet flows in all directions. *Original carpets in impeccable condition.* A giggle rises from my throat as I slip back all those years. My sister and I are rolling in a similar carpet sea, laughing, diving into its luxurious green depths, lost in the churn of imaginary waves. The soft pile enveloping us, supporting us and keeping us warm.

My father, stern at the helm, glares back at us. He tells us to stop, get up, act our age.

"Bloody cold in here." Rob wrinkles his nose. "And musty. Leave the door open for some fresh air." Rob's step is brisk as he heads towards the back of the house.

I step around the room divider and continue to work. *Classic '70s features. Amber-beer-bottle glasswork separates the entranceway from a large, comfortable lounge . . .* Sun-tinged orange light fittings match the glass. *An older-style home with period features.*

I bend down and stroke the carpet's thick pile. It's old but so very soft. So many memories. Winter days and heaters and woolly socks. Scrabble on the loungeroom floor. And ice-cream! There was always ice-cream on a Sunday night when we watched the Sunday movie. I breathe in and smell vanilla. I'm afloat, with my memories, in the sea of green.

"The home was left to the two girls."

I return my focus to the room. My link to the past becomes a whisp of memory.

"They didn't know what to do with it," he says. Keys rattle in his hands; he can't keep still. "Been empty for almost a year." He picks up a carpet deodoriser sitting on the windowsill. I hadn't noticed it until now. "Need to do something before we open—"

The front door slams shut. The amber beer-bottle divider quivers. Rob drops the deodoriser. The scent of pine fills the air. He looks at the door and back at me. In all these years of working together, he's never looked so pale. He squares his shoulders, adjusts his belt.

"Well, at least it smells a bit better," he says, as he puts the container back on the sill. The pile of white powder looks like a mini sand dune. I can't help giggling again.

Rob clears his throat, scuffs the powder. "Better get on with it then." He leaves white footsteps in a path to the front door. "I think I'll wait outside," Rob says, and pulls the door closed behind him.

"Just you and me, hey?"

It's more intimate now Rob's gone. The clock in the entranceway ticks. A tap drips, but it's not from one of the fixtures I've seen. I clutch my pen and notepad tighter. It doesn't feel like I'm alone.

Focusing on the writing, I continue. *Large lounge; original kitchen, green laminate bench; rooms, good-sized and light-filled. Art Deco?* Umm, not quite. I tap my pen, try to draft something in my head as I walk faster through the house, wanting to finish. *Large linen press. Solid-oak polished boards. Bathroom original but clean condition. Three bedrooms, all with BIRs?*

Just one more room to go.

As I approach, the dripping noise slows. The clock's ticks become longer, sluggish. The air thickens, it's harder to breathe. My legs are heavy, as if I'm wading through sludge. Voices disembodied compete like an untuned radio between stations. Each beat of my heart is a separate action. The temperature had dropped, goosebumps prick my skin.

The smell of Old Spice and damp woollen blankets fill the air. I take one more step and enter the final room. A vinyl recliner draped in a multicoloured crotchet rug sits in front of a large window next to a solitary single bed.

He stands beside the chair, ethereal and frail. The carpet in this room is faded, dirty bile-green, worn and threadbare. My pen falls from shaking fingers; my jaw drops too.

He moves to the chair and sits, eyes begging a question I don't understand, then a spasm and he's clutching at his throat, struggling to breathe. *Help me*, he mouths.

I back away. The crackle of static fills the room.

Help me, he repeats, needy and insistent. *Help, help meeeeeeeeeeee.*

Waves of voices roll in and join him, banding together—screaming, roaring, wailing—a tsunami of dissent. Then, as it peaks, the wave breaks in a downpour of despair, crashing against the shore.

And I remember it all.

My father. He was sick. I couldn't help. I was too busy, ignored his calls. He had been drowning too, his lungs filling with fluid. Drowning in his own sea of green.

My notebook is pressed into my stomach, protecting me from pain that's revisited but real. He was so angry and alone, right until the end. We were never able to help him.

"Don't go," dead voices plead, separately and together. I turn away, like—

"—like you did before," they say.

"I'm sorry," I whisper, and run to the door.

Rob's waiting in the carport, but I don't stop. "I'll have it done by tomorrow."

"What about the—?"

"Ring you later."

My car's moving before I've shut the door. Rob runs down the drive, waving, calling out. The car shoots forward, and I'm gripping the wheel to stop my hands from shaking. Emotion wells, grows solid in my throat and all the tears from so long ago are able to release.

At home, I sit at my desk. My workspace is where I bring things to life; it's a place I feel safe. Next to my computer is the photo of my sister and I sitting on the carpet in our lounge room, sailing the calm green sea. Dad sits in his recliner in the corner, reading. It was one of the times I loved. I put the photo down and start to type.

The property listing writes itself. A quick skim and it's almost done. But something's missing—the line that's the kicker, the one that sells the home.

Then I hear it. A whisper.

"Breathe." My father's voice.

This time I don't run. There is a comfort in his voice. I take the breath he couldn't. And another. A warm hand rests upon my shoulder.

This is what we write:

A loving family home. In need of some attention, and a little TLC.

About the Author:

Louise Zedda-Sampson is a Melbourne-based writer, researcher and award-nominated editor, currently living on Bunurong land. You can find Louise at www.louisezeddasampson.com.au and connect with her on Twitter @I_say_meow.

Of Slaves and Lions

Pamela Jeffs

For Aiki.

These ruined gardens were once beautiful. But the wide manicured paths I remember have faded to tracks and the friendly trees have changed. Their crowns look heavy, bristling with dead twigs earned from too many seasons of neglect. I walk with my head down, loath to tarry. The desire to settle a score with the ghosts of my past is my focus. I stride on, hoping to hear them, but they are yet to speak.

An overgrown hedge of bougainvillea bars my way. Bright bunches of purple flowers hang from the vines. Thorns pluck at my sleeves and cheeks as I pass through. The greenery gives way to a clearing and a ring of dead trees. An ancient pond resides at their centre. The silence of the garden stifles. No crickets chirruping, no birdsong. There is only the riot of colourful flowers from overgrown vines and stillness like a neglected graveyard.

The old pond sits dead. The bowl is dry and the low wall surrounding it is all but consumed by a heavily scented jasmine vine. This was my favourite place to play as a child. But alike to that childhood, it has been reduced to bones. I swallow my disappointment. This was the last place I recall being happy. A part of me hoped it had survived. I take a moment to imagine bright fish flitting through the cool water and the vibrancy of the yellow water lilies that once grew here.

Daylight is wasting. Time to continue on if I wish to make the hike back to King's Highway and my horse before dusk. Beyond the trees, the mouldering walls of the old castle rise like broken teeth into the sky—the castle that, long ago, was my home. I am hesitant to approach it. Do I wish to enter there and see again those stones stained with blood? I set aside the horror, remind myself again of my purpose. There must be something of my past—something good—still lingering here.

The pond and its debris-filled bowl falls away behind me. The heady scent of jasmine rises as I disturb the vine. The perfume curls around me, reminding me of warmer, friendlier days filled with sunlight and laughter. The heaviness in my heart eases just a bit.

My reverie is broken. The first sound I've heard in this place since I arrived reaches my ears.

A growl. Low. Fierce.

It comes from the densest part of the shrubbery by the pond, where the greenery covering the wall piles up higher than everywhere else. I ease closer, hesitant. Then I see *her.*

A lioness. She is trapped in a rusted cage—one of the old traps my father's gardener used to set for wolves in the castle grounds. The great cat's eyes gleam, furious. She strikes at the bars. I fall back as her long claws screech down the metal. She retreats to the rear of her prison, her ears held flat to her head and her lips wrinkled back exposing the pointed lengths of her yellow teeth.

How did such a creature find her way into this garden? Then I remember the new king's lion pits located just outside the city; the pits where the underprivileged are tossed when they failed to pay their tithes. Perhaps she came from there; a lioness with a taste for human flesh.

I lean in closer. She snarls a low warning. Her fierce, yellow gaze holds mine conveying a message. *I am a fighter, a survivor. I live beyond the rules men would impose on me.*

Her message resonates.

This cat's soul is a mirror of my own.

And she is abandoned in this palace, just as I once was. My thoughts turn back to the day my childhood ended. At the height of summer, a dry and dusty heat had settled over the gardens. It was the day my father threw away everything. I hadn't understood what it meant when he assembled his soldiers and left through the front gate. But I learnt soon enough. The rebels were coming. And when they arrived, even at the tender age of nine, I saw the truth. My father left us because he feared his own death more than he loved his family and his people. Not that it helped him. The rebel King's forces captured him in the mountains a few months later.

My mother, the Queen, was different. She died the day he left. But I still recall her strength. She had only just hidden me under her bed when the rebels found her. She never betrayed me as they tore the jewels from her neck and ripped her silken gown. And worse. I wish I were more my mother's daughter, but my life has been lived on the edge of a knife—a brutal, hard existence. I am the reverse side of her card. My anger and grief have twisted me. My everyday struggle is to find a place of equanimity.

I brush away the tatters of old memories and the rage they re-awaken. My hope is still to find peace in this return to my childhood home.

The lioness growls again. She wants out, but how to release her? I could leave her here, let her perish. What would be the point of dying trying to save her?

The animal paces. Her yellow hide dapples in the thin sunlight reaching past the thick bars and the jasmine's runaway foliage.

OF SLAVES AND LIONS

Again I am reminded of myself. I paced like that, paced after the rebels captured me and tossed me in a different type of cage—

My decision is made. I'll not leave the cat locked away without a fighting chance.

I'll set her free.

Just like I was set free, albeit scarred and broken and angry. I was saved from my slave-pit cage by the kindness of my father's old gardener. It'd been a long time—ten years since she last saw me—since I was captured and sent to work in the new king's brothels.

She'd paused too when she saw me.

I could smell her fear.

But she handed over the gold to free me.

And like her, I am nothing if not compassionate.

I search for something to loosen the rusted drop-pin holding the door closed. A windfall of weathered branches leaning against the pond looks promising. I pull a thick length of timber free, a length hardened in sunlight and silvered with the passage of years.

It hits the drop-pin with a sharp crack and no luck.

The lioness shies away from the sound, retreating to the far corner of the cage. Her eyes glitter as she watches me—me, the girl who was once a princess, but now just a freed slave with a stick. Malevolence drips from the great cat's stare.

Another hit. The lioness skids to the other side of the cage, her ears flat again. The end of the branch shatters as I miss and connect with the side of the cage. A shower of splinters falls onto the leaf litter below. My palm stings from the backlash, I shake my hand and aim again.

This time I hit the pin with a solid thud. The force of the blow slips it free, letting it fall to the ground in a curtain of rust.

The door creaks open an inch. The lioness's gaze slews sideways to the gap in the cage. I shuffle my grip on the branch, ready to use it as a club if I must.

The lioness pads to the door. Cautious. Her golden hide is crisscrossed with raised ridges of pink flesh, a patchwork of fur and knotted seams. I have seen enough battle scars in my lifetime to recognize the work of a sword at play.

Someone somewhere fought this lioness.

I wonder if they survived.

The great cat hesitates by the door. Her predator's stare follows me—that unblinking gaze of molten gold shot through with black. Taking a breath, I step forward. Slipping the end of my branch through the bars, I pull the door wider. It shrieks on unoiled hinges.

The piercing noise is my undoing. Startled, my attention slips.

The lioness reacts, a streak of gold and muscle flying past the open door and into the ruined garden of my childhood. She skids to a stop behind me, scattering leaf litter and debris across the ground. Her claws are out; thick black hooks that clutch at the earth. Her gaze trains on me, locked like a vice. Her throat ripples. A low growl rolls out into the autumn air.

Perhaps talk will make a difference. "You're free. Go!"

The lioness's growl deepens. Her gaze slips to the club in my hand. The weapon.

I glance at it and then back at her. At her tattered hide and the hatred that burns so bright in her bearing. Realization dawns.

Broken souls are not saved by brutality or bloodshed.

I lean down and place the branch on the ground. The lioness' gaze follows every movement. My hand trembles as I hold it out in front of me, naked.

The dry grass crackles beneath my feet as I move toward the lioness. The tip of my boot scatters a loose stone. Another step. The lioness's haunches bunch. I don't dare pause, afraid my new resolve will waver.

My fingers hover inches away from the great cat. I do not presume to touch, but stand and let her choose to close the distance. My heart hammers in my chest. It's hard to breathe.

I close my eyes and wait. As I do, I realise the garden has awoken. It is full of sound. I focus on the distant birdsong, the crickets and the gentle breeze playing through the trees.

The lioness's touch is tentative at first, just a brush of warmth against my palm. But then she presses harder. I open my eyes. The cat's chin rests in my open hand. Her eyes are on me, but the hate is gone. There is only trust.

I smile, the first genuine one in ten years, and wonder on the strangeness of fate—a fate in which a battered slave tames a savage beast. But perhaps not so strange. It is the lesson my mother died teaching me; that strength is not always about how hard you hit, but how immense your heart can be.

I hold the lioness and turn my gaze to the sky. The broken sunlight kisses my cheeks and with its touch I find resolution.

I have found my ghosts and they have spoken.

About the Author:

Pamela Jeffs is a speculative fiction author from Brisbane, Queensland (Jagera Country) with a love for writing short fiction. She has published three short story collections and has 70+ short stories featured in various national and international magazines and anthologies.

She has been shortlisted for multiple awards throughout her career, including numerous Aurealis Awards and honourable mentions in the Writers of the Future Competition. For more information, visit her at www.pamelajeffs.com.

Faltering

Monique McLellan

For my grandparents.

\#

The signal falters as the train draws into the station. For a moment, there is more than a shadow sitting beside the passenger in the compartment. A green glass lamp casts light over false wood panelling and silk paper. The light is strong, but still there is the shadow of another man, almost there, almost like him. It flickers. It is the kind of thing that would set Amos off, rattling through numbers cardinal, ordinal and theoretical until he has the answer in his teeth—at which point he would pause just long enough for Sula to express her admiration. But Amos is not here, and Sula is long gone.

By the time the passenger is stepping off the carriage, droplets settling in his hair and on his collar as evening draws down the day's fog, the distortion has passed. New photovoltaic lamps on old iron posts, fluted with rust, illuminate the station platform and the square. His shadow stretches, shortens, stretches and shortens exactly as it should while he walks past the rows of lights to the attendant's office to pick up his codes and maps. A sign reads:

Ahenburg, City of the Saved! Baths, Springs and Spa Cures! in fading green paint. Marigolds and roses have been stencilled around the letters.

"Good evening, sir," says the attendant without looking up from a small screen propped beside the service window. He's a small man, spaniel-faced and traditionally vested—a little too charming.

"Good evening, sir," the passenger replies and lets the ensuing silence ripen into a rebuke.

The attendant looks up. His eyes are hazel and bloodshot. A person, then and therefore. The traveller should have guessed. No one would program such a rustic accent. "Oh, no need to call me *sir*, sir. I'm glad to be of service any old how." The attendant taps his screen and asks, "What is your name? What is your number?"

"John Sallourn. Two zero zero nine four two two."

"Another John, then? Another blessed Johannes. Here we are. Please take your network key, sir, and the card for your hotel. Directions are on the back. Is this your first visit to Ahenburg? I can recommend a very fine winstub on Mahler Street—"

"No."

"Not a drinker?"

"No—this isn't my first visit. I've been here before," John says. He peers past the attendant's shingle-sided booth, across the square vanishing in the evening gloom, to pick out the gold-painted letters on the graven street sign. It was bright summer, the last time, and those letters shone like angels had written them. *Place des Lys.* Sula had bought him an ice cream cone from a street vendor set up beneath the plain maple. It had melted all over his fingers.

"Oh. I see. But you're not in the register. An odd thing. But there are glitches from time to time, and yours is a common name. Lots of entries."

"How many?"

"No offence meant, Mr. Sallourn. Welcome to Ahenburg. Please enjoy your stay. Make sure to stay on-network while you're here. Mount Ahen is beautiful, but the upper slopes are still a bit dangerous."

John nods to the station attendant, but the fellow has already turned back to his screen.

* * *

Ahenburg is a handsome stone town. John quickens his pace as the fog thickens, admiring the arching rooflines and frescoes even as they blur behind the worsening weather. Network receptors are furled under the eaves so that he can barely see them—but there must be twice as many as needed, blinking so faintly that his unenhanced vision can barely perceive them. Red geraniums nod in window boxes along the crooked streets. Quiet streets. No buzzing neon, no supra-electric whir. Were it not for the half-hidden receptors and the smell of nitrogen fixer on the wind, he could be walking into a different age.

No. That isn't true. He wishes he were doing just that, still sticky-fingered with rosewater ice-cream, just a boy hopping at the hem of Sula's yellow dress. It is bloody obvious that this town is just a tourist trap, painted like a postcard in gingerbread brown and wine-bottle green. Just outside the old centre, network glitches glimmer where the protocol shifts from residential settings to high-security geo-mapping. The light reflects in the low clouds—white, green, green, blue. Ripples of electrostatic discharge. But in the rain and mist, he could pretend.

John reaches the hotel. No one in the lobby, no one in the bar. Two problems for a man chasing a memory. He logs his codes in the network port beside the elevator, then pauses. There is a room upstairs, reserved and prepared for him. A shower, clean sheets, a door he can lock against the world. His left side has gone numb with fatigue. A row of faded scars run from just below his jaw, notching the flesh every few centimetres, until they stop just above the swell of his left knee. These scars are straight, and precise, but they still cause him pain.

FALTERING

He goes back to the hotel bar, finds the switch for the lights and turns them on. They flicker once and settle. Reflections play on the thick glass bottles that line the shelves behind the counter, traditional neurotoxins with quaint labels bearing pictures of carts and castles. Spirits. He checks his watch—ten past ten, and three unread messages from Amos. Not too late to ring for assistance. The port in the lobby crackles. There is a momentary delay as the signal catches and catches again, and a wan-faced girl emerges from the darkness between blinks. She's a real person, cast from somewhere nearby. The image is crisp. The look in her eyes is baleful.

"Good evening, sir. How can I help you? Drinks? Help yourself to the sesame liquor. It's the off season and we've ordered too much of the stuff for the locals and the ghosts."

John smiles despite his aches. He just has to imagine that he's on the boards again, and the globes above the bar are scoop lights above a stage. "A drink would be welcome. What do you recommend for—"

"The sesame stuff. As I just said. On the left, second shelf up. Weren't you listening? It'll do the job."

John nods. His shadow, shrunken and faint, shrugs. He takes down a bottle of the sesame pastis and pours himself a thimbleful. It is clear and tinged with grey. He might have guessed it was poison.

A thrum against the underside of his wrist suggests that Amos has sent him a fourth message. He does not check.

The barkeep raises an eyebrow at him as the moment drags. She asks, "Will that be all?"

"Ahem. Hmm. Well. And the ghosts? You mentioned ghosts?"

She gives him a hard look. She is quite young under the disgruntlement that sets her face in such sharp angles. "You're not a journalist, are you? Because that was all dust and wind. Miscommunication. Nothing happened."

"Do I look like a journalist?"

"You've looked twice in every corner of this room. Yes."

"But I'm not. A journalist, I mean to say. I was an actor. My Polonius was much admired."

The barkeep does not seem appreciative. John tries not to quail. He does wonder, sometimes, whether there was any point to the sighing and speechifying. He spent half a lifetime chasing his shadow around a stage, never catching it.

"Have another drink and get some sleep, Mr. Vagabond. No more questions."

"Are you this genial with all your guests, Miss?"

"Only the ones who log false codes. Yours are seventy-nine years old. You're not quite decrepit enough to match."

"Thank you, I suppose."

"Wasn't a compliment. You're lucky if I don't turn you in."

FALTERING

John drinks his thimbleful of alcohol. It is strong and too sweet. The muscles at the back of his neck unwind and his aches fade. Reminded of rosewater ice and sticky fingers, he climbs upstairs to sleep in a room that might once have been a cupboard, with a small window shut against the night and the rainstorm.

* * *

The sharp song of a blackbird, a melodious battle cry, wakes him late the next morning. His cravat is knotted too closely around his neck. He takes it off and does not replace it. After a quick wash in lukewarm water, John puts his rumpled clothes back on without checking his watch. This is a holiday, after all.

He has earned a holiday. Some time for himself. Even great-hearted Sula has gone her own way. Saying his farewells to her at the taxi rank near St. V's with a quick kiss on the cheek, he did not realise it would be the last time. Her skin was like onion paper under his lips. She was a bit paler than usual, perhaps, but her condition was not obvious. She told him, "I do not want to be fixed."

Eating breakfast from a foil packet, he walks back into the town centre. Egg proteins catch in his teeth, but he has lost too much of the day to sit down for tea and crumpets.

Ahenburg is not quite as charming under the spotlight of April sunshine. Some of the frescoes are printed plywood. Some of the carved timber shutters are polymers moulded to look like cedar. Despite careful restoration, layers of paint and plaster, some buildings still bear smoke stains in shades of brown and grey. If he strives, John can catch a whiff of ash and brimstone.

Or maybe that's his imagination again.

He is careful to meander like a tourist, stopping at a tobacco shop to pick up the newspapers; special editions printed on synthetic cellulose with a paperish texture and grain. The day's headlines and by-lines are displayed in black, white and red. There is no mention of him. As expected, of course. Many years have passed since he was fit for page 27, tucked behind the news of Old Yian losing another match. He reminds himself that this suits him as he browses the lightwood carvings of Mount Ahen, painted with race-car-red lava spilling down her slopes. A holographic card catches his eye. It shows the mountain shaking, then swelling sidewards until the peak starts to crumble. A gout of pale spume and vapour surges up into a sparkling grey sky. No lava to be seen. He flips the card to reset the recording.

* * *

It is not quite noon, the sun high above and glinting off the meteorological grid in the upper troposphere, when John stops dithering. Partway between the market square and the old cathedral, he slips down an alleyway. The back street is little more than a split between two buildings, strewn with plastic bins and the refuse of a nearby café. Emerging into another alley, he steps over a gutter green with algae and sidles past empty doorways and fire-scarred stones, discarded vegetable peelings and stripped, past-date network jacks. This is backstage, in the wings, in the flies, and John can see the way the ropes cross and the pulleys squeak behind the painted scene.

He comes back out into the sunshine on a small grassy ridge at the edge of town. Beyond an old tanner's ditch full of dark water and reeds, there is a meadow spread with brilliant flowers. Violets and bluebells and daisies on a bed of black, black dust. Above the meadow stands Mount Ahen. It does not loom as it should. It is a modest cap of dark rock, elliptical, its edge fringed with pale vegetation.

John scans the mountain for ghosts as he walks towards it, but discerns none. Disappointing. It would have been a thrill to see shades of people from before the eruption and the reset, even if they were only faulty recordings.

The buzz and click of network failure are, however, discernible even to his unenhanced hearing. Not quite decrepit. Lights are flickering far above him, parallels in colours he can't quite see.

With some scrambling, he clears the tanner's ditch and strides into the meadow. There are a hundred excuses for trespassing—it's a fine day for a picnic, it's such a beautiful view—and he has practised an expression of harmless impudence to present to any challengers. Surely someone will stop him any second . . . But no one does. Has he been lucky? Has time and lassitude made the locals careless? Perhaps the rumours of danger are overblown.

But has he walked this way before? John cannot be sure. It has been more than sixty years and the land has shifted, centimetre by centimetre, until every centimetre is different. Human bodies are thus, as well. The old cells dwindle and new ones take their place until the bones soften and the brain blinks out. The only thing you keep is your shadow, if that.

Even if he discounts Amos' meddling and the many costume changes of the intervening decades, John is not the child who once traipsed up this slope, trying to outdistance Amos and Sula as they paraded, arm-in-arm, under ancient trees. He affected a great interest in butterflies so that he did not have to listen to them whispering. There are no butterflies today. Perhaps the extended network scares them off. Amos would know the answer, but Amos is not here.

John is approaching the edge of that network. In a few hundred paces, he will be beyond the split-second comms and the weather grid. His heart will beat at its own speed and his appetites will rise and subside without feeding data into his watch and sending him polite, priggish messages to slow down, sit down, breathe. Breathe. This path is steeper than it used to be, if it is indeed the same path.

FALTERING

He cannot be sure, but he thinks he's on the right track. The flowers are different—the trees are different too, short shaggy clusters of hawthorn and laburnum—but the view back towards Ahenburg is as it should be.

* * *

The last time he came here—the first time he came here—he was young, unhappy and wished to be alone. So he was a fair way uphill of Amos and Sula when he saw something arc into the sky—maybe a rocket, a childhood fascination—but then low grey clouds were gathering and rushing downhill.

Sound arrived later, moving slower than fear, so John was already running by the time he heard cracking and howling many times greater than thunder. Blind with panic, he could not see the environmental grid flicker and fail. No memories of pain are left to him, but it must have hurt. Nor does he remember Amos coming back for him, searching through choking fog at the splintered edges of a broken system—but he must have, or John would not have survived.

Afterwards, in a hotel function room turned field hospital, Sula held him close and said that he was lucky. She traced her fingers down the row of incisions along his left side, where the receptors and emitters were inserted. Cutting-edge, said Amos, smiling in that way he imagined was fatherly. A prototype which could mean the end of sickness and pain and disfigurement. Amos always meant well.

* * *

John reaches the edge of the network. Ahead of him lies more meadow, more midges, and a thickening hawthorn copse. Mistletoe and weeds. Now or never. He steps beyond, leaving his shadow behind to stretch downhill, the shape of a man, distended.

The skin on his left side flinches. There is no outward sign of change, but he feels the years catch him all at once. Sixty-three blows to his heart, to his gut. It does hurt. He thinks of turning back. Of Sula, young and lovely in her yellow dress. Rosewater ices, gold-etched letters, the plywood painted like frescoes. The end of sickness and pain and disfigurement. Sula standing at the taxi rank near St. V's, clutching her coat so that the wind could not pull it open as she said, "I do not want to be fixed."

Each step is more difficult than the last. John continues uphill, toward the volcano, wondering how far he will get before he falls. Setting his teeth, he resolves to find out. His gums, of all things, sting. There is blood on his tongue. The taste surprises him, after so long.

About the Author:
Monique is a writer and translator living in Melbourne, on Wurundjeri land.

Maki

Nikky Lee

To Megan, for your courage, honesty and the raw emotion you penned to paper. Your stories will stay with me forever.

#

I wake in the middle of the night to the call. It echoes through the walls of our shack, over the rumble of the retreating tide. I lie there in the dark, hot and sticky in the muggy night, sheets tangled about my legs, sure I've misheard, until it comes again.

A creaking whistle from the beach, like the squeak of our rusted front gate. But the direction is wrong, sound not quite right. The breeze carries it over the dunes, across our back porch, and I am up, out of bed, pulling the window open. Cool air laps my fingers. Darkness peers back. No stars are out; a halo of cloud-diffused light is the only sign of the moon. I wait, counting the seconds.

The cry comes again, louder, pulling at my gut. Something is wrong. I glance back to the bed at Ari, still asleep, his snores blending into the white noise of the sea. Oblivious. As always.

Another wail and I'm in the kitchen, fumbling under the sink for the emergency torch. At the fridge I pause, hesitating over the notepad stuck to the door. I teeter; last night's argument still simmers inside me, warring against common sense. A fresh cry bleeds through the night. With a huff, I snatch a pen from the drawer, pull the pad off the fridge, and scrawl a message.

Gone for a walk.

The letters are sharp and jagged, waiting to bite. I snatch up my phone and stumble out onto the porch, flicking the torch on as I set off through the scrub; down the well-worn track that has borne a stream of friends and family to the waters. At the crest of the final dune, I stop, eyes adjusting in the dark to make out a shape on the sand. I kick off my jandals and run.

Under the torchlight lies a patchwork of white and black. An orca. Maki, as Ari would say. I push the thought of him away. Maki moans as I draw near, flails its head, air rushing from its blowhole. I crouch over him, run a hand over damp skin, feeling puckered scars and divots from a long life at sea.

"Why are you here?" I whisper. "Are you hurt?" I flash the light down the beach, clumps of seaweed mark the lines of the withdrawing tide, all the way to the water's edge fifty meters way. It won't be in again until morning. I swear under my breath, look the whale in the eye.

You owe me for this.

I take out my phone and dial. The line rings out. "Come on," I mutter, and dial again. This time, Ari's groggy voice answers.

"Lin?" A pause, and I imagine his hand falling on the empty sheets beside him. "Where are you?" An edge of panic creeps into his voice. "Are you all right?"

"Call help, there's an orca on the beach."

He comes down half an hour later, carrying buckets and towels. "It will take them hours to reach us," he says. "They said to keep it wet." His eyes slide away from my face. I hope he feels guilty. He should. He should have asked first. Taken a moment to consider what saying 'yes' might mean for me. For us.

We drape towels over Maki's back, pour water on his skin. He cries make up for our silence. His song rings into the night, and far off, a chorus echoes across the water. My skin prickles. His pod is calling.

Ari and I work, side by side, digging a trench between Maki and the sea. Maki doesn't flail anymore. His head lulls on the sand. "Hold on," I tell him. "The tide is coming. Just a little longer."

Ari pours a bucket over him, massages the waters in. "Don't give up on us," he whispers. "Not yet."

My gut wrenches. *Don't let it end now.*

We consign ourselves to wait. Ari's hand closes around mine, our wet and gritty fingers lacing together as we sit beside the whale. My husband hums under his breath. I stroke Maki's nose.

"I'm sorry," he says into the torchlight. "I know you love it here; love the work you do at the conservation centre." He swallows. "I'll turn down the offer." His voice is tight, strained. The sound of a dream smothered, and I suddenly hate myself, hate the words that came spitting out of me hours ago. *What about me? What about what I want?* Selfish words, but I can't brush them aside or put them to bed like they don't matter.

Maki huffs from the sand, one dark eye fixed longingly on the sea.

I rest my head on Ari's shoulder. "I'm sorry too." Beyond the breakers, Maki's pod calls again, distant, a family torn apart. "Would they let you work remote?" I ask, then bite my lip, swallow, and add: "Or fly in, fly out?" I hate the idea of having him gone for days at a time, but even more, I hate the thought of him sacrificing his dream for mine.

Ari is quiet as he weighs my words. "I'll ask," he says at last, and squeezes my hand. "For us."

Dim light finds us like that as the first trickle of the returning tide laps my toes.

"Ari, the sea!" We dig in fervour, channelling the water to our ward. Maki is quiet. The tide seeps in, surging about our ankles, then our knees. We unearth the sand from under him, freeing his fins as the water ebbs and flows. As one we push, but Maki doesn't budge.

"Come on," I plead.

"Let's go bud," Ari says. "Just a little more."

Our words don't reach him. A wave swamps us up to our waists, clinging my pyjamas around my legs.

Then Maki's pod calls again; clicks and kees swirl around us. Maki twitches, like a child coming awake. He bucks and twists, tail slapping the water. Bit by bit, his bulk shifts. Ari and I sink our weight against his head and shove. We move. Sand grinds under our feet, slides under Maki's belly, every centimetre growing easier.

We guide him out. Cold washes against my skin, against Ari's, against Maki's. In the distance, engines rumble over the dunes: help arriving. Hands join ours, pushing, lifting, steering.

He is free.

We release our hold, and Maki floats there for one, two puffs of his blowhole. He rolls onto his side, dark eyes meeting mine. For a heartbeat, I'm lost in them, before his bulbous nose nods.

"Thank you."

The sentiment shivers through me. Not quite words. And not quite of my own making. An intake of breath tells me Ari's heard it too. He clutches my hand. Squeezes.

Then, with a sweep of fins and a slap of his tail, Maki returns to the deep.

On the shore, Ari wraps an arm around me, our warmth soaking into one another. His lips brush my forehead. "I love you."

About the Author:

Nikky Lee is an award-winning author who grew up as a barefoot 90s kid in Perth, Western Australia on Whadjuk Noongar Country. She now lives in Aotearoa New Zealand with a husband, a dog and a couch potato cat. In her free time she writes speculative fiction, often burning the candle at both ends to explore fantastic worlds, mine asteroids and meet wizards.

She's had over two dozen stories published in magazines, anthologies and on radio. Her debut novel, The Rarkyn's Familiar—*an epic tale of a girl bonded to a monster—will be published by Parliament House Press in 2022.*

*Website: www.nikkythewriter.com | Facebook: /nikkythewriter
Twitter: @NikkyMLee | Instagram: @NikkyMLee*

Tox Hunt

Tim Borella

This is dedicated to Dominique, a brave and beautiful soul.

#

It was a good spot we found that time round, and I felt more confident than I had in a long time that we'd be able to stay for a season, maybe more. We'd walked for days, pushing northwest to get up into the hills and well away from any tracks that looked like they'd been used in the past year or so. We slept wherever we found ourselves at sunset, eating sparingly so we didn't use up our stores too quick. Mum had to take everything edible out of Rowie's pack and dole it out to him bit by bit when he just couldn't go any longer without something, him being at that stage where he just needed to grow no matter what. I'd try to sneak him some of mine when I could, but Mum wouldn't have it.

"You need it just as much as he does, Connie," she'd say, with a meaningful glance at my chest which made me squirm.

"You've got a lot going on in that body of yours too. If anyone's going to go without, it's got to be us," meaning the adults. She and Dad had been able to keep going on barely anything, but I was getting more concerned about Granddad as time went by. He'd always been so strong and fearless, but lately, he was just that bit slower to climb over a fallen log or get up after a break from walking, wincing and looking around to check no-one had seen. I had, though.

We came across the hut mid-morning. I saw it first and whistled softly. Dad motioned for everyone to crouch, slid his pack off and crept forward to take a look. We were well hidden, but I couldn't see what Dad was doing. After what felt like an hour he returned, walking upright, and I knew there wasn't any danger. Everyone relaxed and stood up, massaging stiff muscles.

"Abandoned," Dad said. "I don't reckon anyone's been there for years. All right for a while, I'd say."

The hut sat on a little flat spot on the side of a ridge, made of logs and slabs from the trees around it. It was rough and simple, a rectangle divided into two smaller areas, with a rough mudbrick fireplace and chimney that was half falling apart. Compared to what we were used to it was a palace, with a roof that kept the rain out and a proper wooden floor. On the other side of the ridge ran a permanent creek which widened into a couple of nice little pools where you could wash and get water easily.

There were animals around too, kangaroo and rabbit, and tracks that might have been from the tiny mammoths that were said to have spread into the wilder parts of the state. I'd never seen them, but I secretly fantasised I might be able to catch one and tame it. They were a bit like us, outside the natural order of things.

We set snares in likely places, using scraps of food as bait but also rubbing our sweat in the loops. It didn't cost anything and was a quick, sure kill for a few creatures that we knew of— certain bandicoots and marsupial mice, some birds. And the twenty percent of humans that were vulnerable to it, of course, which was why they were hunting us.

Mum and Dad scoped out the area while Rowie, Granddad and I set up the sleeping gear and got water. As it was getting dark, we gathered around to sit, eat and go through the plan. Listening to the quiet bush sounds, I felt I could fall asleep right there.

"Are you with us, Con?" Dad asked gently, and I shook my head to clear the cobwebs.

"Sorry," I mumbled.

He reached over and ruffled my hair. "I know, sweetheart. But we have to get this done."

I nodded and listened hard, thinking the words in my head as he said them. They'd been drummed into us so many times. If we weren't a hundred percent clear on what to do when—not if—they came, it wouldn't just be that one killed, it'd be all of us.

"First thing if there's a contact, Rowie—what is it?" said Dad.

"We hide where we are."

"Good boy. And what if someone gets found?"

"Everyone else keeps hiding."

Dad paused, looking around at us all in the half-light as if it was already happening.

"And what if they see us all?" he continued.

"We scatter," we all said, like it was a prayer.

* * *

A memory comes to me, clear as clear. It's maybe ten days after we got to the hut and I'm in the creek, scrubbing months of mud out of my pants. My shirt's spread out on the grass to dry and I'm in just my underwear. The sun soaks my back and neck, and I pause and look around the clearing. My breathing and heartbeat are slow. In a lifetime of running, this is maybe the first time I've been truly relaxed. An unfamiliar word pops into my mind. Home.

There was plenty of food if you knew where to look, and as weeks passed we slipped into a pattern of living as old as the human race, trapping and fishing and gathering seeds and roots. Rowie and I explored our territory, following animal paths through the scrubby undergrowth and finding burrows and snake holes among tree roots, nests where there might be eggs, native beehives in dead stumps.

We were never careless. We always assumed—by habit so long-established it had become instinct—that danger was waiting around every corner, over every crest. At the hut, we all took turns at lookout, with at least one awake at all times. Mum and Dad took the night shifts mostly, but Granddad and I did some too. Now and then when Rowie couldn't sleep he'd come out and find me, making just enough noise so I could hear him and quietly call him over to my hiding place. We'd look out into the darkness together, sometimes talking softly but always vigilant. He was nearly ten, turning from my little brother into someone more thoughtful, more real to me somehow.

"How could people be so stupid?" he asked me on one of those nights. I knew what he meant. He'd been talking with Granddad, asking questions just like I had when I'd gotten old enough to figure out what I needed to ask.

We were here now because people were dumb and vain and didn't know how badly what they were playing with could hurt them. The way Granddad told it, people in his parents' time lived like spoilt children, expecting everything—food, water, comfort, entertainment—to just be there, and that their easy lives would go on like that forever.

But even though they had everything, it wasn't enough. They worked out how to meddle with their genes so their children could be more beautiful, taller, have some particular colour hair or eyes. We were like we were because my great-great-grandparents—and plenty of others of their generation—chose to give their children the gift of *smelling nice*. Instead, the gift turned out to be those children's children having sweat that was deadly poison to one in five people who came into contact with it.

Meanwhile the world was getting more and more dangerous, and the governments who were supposed to be keeping people safe were losing control. They were protecting themselves and pretending everything was fine even as food and water ran out and the whole shaky system began to collapse.

Kids like Granddad were snatched away by soldiers and police and never seen again or just killed in cold blood by scared people, but his parents didn't let that happen. They fled to remote places so they could survive off the land and give their kids a chance of making it to adulthood. Other families like his had done the same, and over the years crossed paths with each other and built cautious alliances. Sickness and hunters took their toll, but babies were also born into that rough existence—babies like us. Not all had the condition—Mum didn't—but mostly it bred true. Even those it skipped were carriers, so we were all tainted with the legacy, all running from the hatred.

* * *

That last night I was on watch, a few hours before dawn. There was no moon and everything was still and clear, one of those nights when the stars burned bright and I could imagine we were the only people on earth. It was nice to think that, and I suppose I'd even slipped into a kind of delusion that we were safe, that we could just live there in that valley and be left alone.

Then, I heard it—the bark of a dog, one sharp sound cutting the silence, then nothing. I went cold all over, straining to hear more. It was some distance away, but how far was hard to tell. Not a dingo, a hunting dog. I got up and hurried as quickly and quietly as I could to the hut. Dad was already at the door to meet me, a shadow gripping my arm as I came in.

"You heard that?" he whispered.

"Yes," I said. There was no need for more.

Everyone else was stirring, and Dad said the words that made it real.

"We have to move, now."

We'd all let our guard down without knowing it. Everything should have been packed except the sleeping gear, but we were all bumbling around in the dark finding bits and pieces, shoving them into our packs. Not until we were out the door and ready to move did a terrible sinking feeling hit my guts. My main responsibility.

"The waterskins!" I blurted out, realising I'd left them at the creek the afternoon before. I'd seen and tried unsuccessfully to stalk a wallaby, getting caught up in the chase and ending up forgetting to go back and get the skins. So stupid.

"We're going to need them," Mum said. The dismay in her voice was clear. We each had a litre or two of water in our packs, but that wouldn't be enough on the run unless we were very lucky. The country had been drying out and water sources were scarce.

"I'll get them and meet you at the First Place," I said. Dad began to protest but I cut him off. "Nobody else will find them in the dark. It's my fault, so I should fix it."

"You're right, Con, but I'm coming with you," said Mum. "We'll meet them there." She hugged the others and turned to me, hitching up her pack.

Just then, another bark rang out from the direction we'd first entered the valley, closer than before. This was it.

"Come on," said Dad, and with that, he, Granddad and Rowie were gone, moving away in single file.

For a moment I just stood there, frightened, then gathered my courage and began to pick my way up and over the ridge, making for the creek. Mum followed close behind.

* * *

Two hours later we were nearing the First Place, a small clearing four or five kilometres from the hut near a big sandstone bluff where the creek took a sharp bend. The full waterskins weighed down on our shoulders as we picked our way up a small rise and crouched in the bush near the top to wait for dawn. We'd heard no more barking or signs of pursuit, and as the light crept back into the world, a whipbird's call broke the silence. Mum and I looked at each other, relieved—that was the signal, and in the half-light three figures emerged from the tree line below, two tall and one shorter. As Mum went to stand movement to the right caught my eye. I grabbed her arm and pulled her back down as two other people burst into the clearing, shouting and brandishing guns. We watched, helpless, as Dad, Granddad and Rowie turned to run the other way, only to be blocked by two more hunters, one holding the leash of a straining dog.

The hunters closed in. The men jeered as Dad stood head down, defeated. Then, in one fluid motion, he dropped his pack and ran full tilt at the closest one, lunging for the gun and taking him to the ground in a crunching hit. Then Mum was up and running too, careening down the slope. I froze for a second, tensing to follow, when two shots rang out. Dad slumped in a heap and Mum tumbled headlong down the last few metres to lie still. I screamed and rose to run to them, but the crack and splinter of wood next to my head forced me back into cover. More shots came and I crashed away through the bush, hating myself for not going back but knowing there was nothing I could do. *Scatter*, I thought over and over, *we scatter.*

I ran as hard and as far as I could until I had to stop, bent over and gasping great breaths, willing the pounding in my ears to subside so I could hear if they were following. My clothes were torn and I had cuts and grazes all over me. I'd dropped all my gear, and thought about backtracking to try to at least find some of the water, but the distant sound of the dog's barking made up my mind - I had to keep running. Perhaps if I lost them I could get to the second meeting place and just hope Granddad or Rowie had somehow gotten away, but I already knew that wouldn't happen. Crying bitter tears for my poor family—and myself—I continued in an exhausted plod, trying to put distance behind me.

I don't remember much else from that day except stumbling along with no clear direction, the afternoon's heat making my head swim and magnifying the primal thirst that was becoming my sole focus. By evening I still hadn't found any water. I have a dim memory of crawling in among some thorny bushes, then, nothing more.

Sometime in the early morning, odd sounds roused me, and I forced my eyes open to see the dog's sleek black muzzle thrusting towards me, held back by the taut lead. I tried to push back further under the bushes, snagging myself on the stems, but it was useless. I was done.

"Come out, tox," said a voice.

"Come and get me," I said, numb from fatigue, thirst and grief and past caring what happened to me. The dog pulled sideways, trying to get at me from another direction, and I saw the hunter's face. He wasn't much older than I was, and though his expression gave nothing away, what I saw didn't look like hatred.

He took something from his belt and I flinched as he threw it towards me. It skidded to a stop by my feet and I stared at it in disbelief—a water bottle. I was too thirsty to care if it was some cruel joke. I grabbed it and drank.

"The boy," he said. "He's still alive."

Alive! Relief hit like a punch to my chest. All resistance drained from me and I lay in the dust and cried.

* * *

That young hunter could have killed me, but instead chose to let me go. Perhaps he realised that—just like me—he had no say about what kind of life he'd been born into, but could still decide what to make of it. His dog was well-trained, and he had allowed it to bark, to warn us. He told me his family would collect a bounty for my dead parents and grandfather, but my brother would be taken to a camp in the south. He didn't know what they did there, but he told me how I could find it.

* * *

The compound is fenced and guarded, and though I've been watching long enough to know the guards are lazy and there might be ways to get in and even out again, it's a huge step from knowing that to getting up from this hiding place and moving out down the hill to do . . . I don't know what. Half of me wants to just melt away through the trees and go back to running, but I can't do that. If my brother is here, we'll leave together. Or not at all.

About the Author:

Tim Borella is an Australian author, mainly of short speculative fiction published in anthologies, online and in podcasts. He lives in beautiful Far North Queensland in an area recognised as the traditional lands of the Ngadjon-jii people. For more information, visit his Tim Borella – Author page on Facebook.

Three Tasks for the Sidhe

Leanbh Pearson

*For Jan and Jane, beloved storytellers both. And in memory of
Aiki, mentor and friend.*

#

There would never be a ballad sung about the three tasks you
and Fianait endured. As a minstrel, you might have composed
your own, but that right was taken from you and only those who
witnessed your challenge to the Fair Folk, know the truth of
your tale. Though there are countless songs of mortal men who
loved a lady of the Sidhe, none loved Fianait as she did you: a
love to endure.

* * *

You and Fianait would meet in secret when the Fair Folk
walked the mortal realm, those liminal hours be'twixt day and
night. Hidden in dense bracken, clinging vine, and shadowed
woodland, you would wait, watching those lords and ladies
dance in the half-light, then follow Fianait from the grove into

darker reaches of the forest. She who among us, was always drawn to the meadows at the forest edges. You were a harpist, a minstrel and singer of the oldest songs, you knew the tales of mortal men obsessed with the ladies of the Sidhe. For Fianait was unlike any mortal woman just as she was unlike any among the Folk. Although the daughter to the Winter Lord, she was unnatural, too often drawn to the forest fringe, her gaze lost to the horizon.

Yet your eyes never wavered from Fianait, her simple gown of moonlight and dew, unadorned by the gems of starlight that hung around the graceful necks of her ladies, their gowns spun of spider silk, laced with hoarfrost and dew. You saw none but Fianait when you met that fateful time at the forest edge. She, turning to you; her violet eyes tinted with the blue of an evening sky.

"Fianait," you breathed, taking her slender form in your arms.

Her smile was summer itself, all warmth and gentleness, fit to make the Queen of the Summer enraged if she had witnessed it. "We should not meet here anymore," she murmured.

"Why?" you asked. "Why hide the love I bear you?"

She frowned then, delicate brows knitting, considering your words as she glanced back towards the dancing Fae.

"Leave with me, Fianait," you begged.

Perhaps you had never intended it to be serious, but once those words had left your lips they found a truth of their own.

When your gaze met Fianait's violet eyes, that truth sunk roots of its own, deep into the earth and she.

She shook her head, black ringlets cascading around her shoulders, hiding her face from you. "I cannot leave with you. You know the laws of my kind. You know who my father is."

"They're still dancing," you pressed, glancing back towards the grove, the gowns and frock coats of the Sidhe glittering in the predawn light. "Your father need not know."

"You forget, I am not my own mistress in these woods."

"You can't leave freely?" you asked, taking her pale hand in yours. "You are bound to your father's court?"

"We are beholden to our courts," she said. "If I am to leave with you, my father must release me."

"Then let me speak with him," you said, noticing several handmaidens now standing in the shadows.

"There is naught but tragedy awaiting you," she insisted. "But I release you, mortal. Leave these woods and our court to their moonlit revelries."

"Fianait, you never entrapped me. No magic bonds our love that is not of the purest kind. But I *will* take my leave if you answer one question."

Her bottom lip trembled, and she hesitated. Tendrils of hoarfrost uncurled across the forest floor and Fianait stared as dew froze along each stem and leaf. Reluctantly, she bowed her head in subservience, the Lord of the Winter approaching in near silence.

"Daughter," he said. "Introduce me to our mortal guest?"

Fianait lowered her eyes when her father spoke, then lifted her violet gaze to meet your own. "This is Matthew, a mortal man dear to me and one with whom I would leave our realm."

The Winter Lord's lips curled in contempt, and he glared at you, an intruder to his predawn revels. But resigned, he sighed, ejecting a puff of frozen air into the shadowy space between you and Fianait. "You trespass on my Court tonight, mortal," he spoke, revealing pointed teeth. "Does my daughter speak the truth? Do you seek to take one beholden to me?"

"The Lady Fianait speaks the truth, our hearts are bound together," you said, fists clenched, willing bravery into your words. "I would seek to fasten her hand to mine and take her from this realm as my wife."

Those still dancing among the dew and muted light now scattered at your words, their dance abandoned as the grove shivered with unspoken anticipation. The dispersed dancers peered from the half-shadow, eyes bright with interest.

Fianait stood motionless opposite you, brilliant eyes pleading where her lips would not betray her. She knew you were a skilled harpist, that very calling as a minstrel had led you to these woods the first time, searching for truth in the oldest lores about the Fae. In those tales and legends of the Sidhe, where trickery and ill-bargains were made, you now knew the ground you walked upon was slick with ice, a single mis-step would crack it and plunge you into peril.

"No mortal may challenge a claim on those beholden to me," the Winter Lord said, dark eyes glittering.

"Yet Fianait is our daughter," spoke the Winter Queen, her bare feet soundless on the frosty ground as she stopped beside her Lord. "It is prudent that Fianait discover how poor her choice of a mortal lover is, the weakness of his kind. If he seeks a hand-fasting with Fianait, let him prove the strength of their love."

The Winter Lord bowed in agreement to his Queen, then turned his black eyes on you. "Complete three tasks to my satisfaction without Fianait's aid, witnessed here by the Winter Court, and I will concede for Fianait to be your wife and she might leave our realm with you at dawn."

Glancing to Fianait, you met her gaze, an unspoken agreement passing between you. You wet your lips and declared your acceptance of the challenge put before you.

The Winter Lord bowed with rigid formality and, raising his hands, palms to the night sky, he flexed his long fingers as though clawing the air. The ground trembled, then pulled apart, saplings tearing from the soil, reaching skyward like twiggy fingers, mirroring those beseeching hands cast to the sky. Strengthening his command over the natural elements, the saplings grew with an uncanny speed, entwining their limbs, until a thorny arch awaited you.

"Your first task." The Winter Queen gestured to the hawthorn arch. "Only a love that is true and strong can stand beneath the thorns."

Paling, you tried to conceal your unease. You knew the old songs, those ancient tales of men broken beneath hawthorns and ensorcelled by the Fair Folk. Recognising the unmasked fear in Fianait's eyes—before she could protest, and your cowardice might lure you away—you walked beneath the thorny arch.

There was little space to stand without rounding your shoulders, exposing your back to the woody limbs above. The Winter Lord inclined his head once to his Queen, who moving directly into your sight, raised her hands. Somewhere behind you, Fianait gave a piteous moan, the sound of her anguish nearly unmanning you. Shoulders tensed, you waited, body pressed against the boughs above. Hawthorn roots encircled your boots, creeping, thorny vines holding you in firm. A slow, tremulous groan shuddered through the branches above, the wood sounding as if it were constricting, drawing itself inward to crush your bones.

Then, without warning, those slender hawthorn branches disentangled from the arch, unfolding limbs, long black thorns lining their length. The Winter Queen gestured, and rapid whip-like branches moved as though extensions of her body. They lashed your exposed shoulders, arms and back, slicing through leather jerkin, shirt beneath and cutting bloody marks across your skin. A scream, ragged and piteous, broke your lips but you only bowed your shoulders, covered your unprotected eyes and face beneath your hands. Even as tears mingled with blood, and thorny blows struck you again and again, your refusal to fail Fianait remained unwavering.

The Winter King sighed and halted the blows. Pain lanced through your broken skin, the rawness of nerves exposed to air sent shivers of shock through you as if the thorns still lashed you.

"The second task is not as easy," the Winter Lord snarled. "You would not be the first mortals to value love until its absence."

Without comment, the Winter Queen gestured again and two handmaidens hurried forward, taking your already bleeding arms, and dragged you before her. Despite your earlier bravado, fear slivered inside you like a chill, and now, standing before the Winter Queen, your resolve began to fail. Before you could turn aside, her slender fingers tightened around your wrist, impossibly strong, like manacles that held you fast. Where she touched you, the skin burned with cold, icy tendrils spreading over you—shivers racking your body like the height of fever—your breath in hollow rasps. Then as numbness overwhelmed the pain, the callousness of the second task became clear, and you stared at the ruin of your harpist's hand – those once dextrous fingers unable to break your grip with the queen even as sensation returned. Looking at the imprint of her grip indelibly marked in black frost-bitten flesh, you met her dark eyes and refused to flinch.

"Has he completed the second task to satisfaction?" Fianait asked.

"Two tasks have been completed," the Winter Lord said. "But in life, as beyond death, love is an eternal flame that cannot be extinguished. Complete my third task and your love will be worthy of Fianait."

Discontent to watch you suffer but powerless to offer aid under the bindings of this bargain, Fianait struggled against her handmaidens, and breaking free, ran into the centre of the clearing. There, holding you in her embrace, she pleaded for mercy. Easing Fianait's wretched sobs, you glanced at the blue-grey flesh of your right arm, an agonising memento of the Winter Queen's frigid touch.

Consoling Fianait, you stepped away from her embrace to stand before the Winter Lord and his Queen. A tremor of fear shook your limbs as the Queen raised her hands once more. Between her outstretched fingers, a golden chalice appeared, its shining form hovering in the space before you. Long hours spent memorising the old tales gave you forewarning of what was to come. But, with trembling hands, you took the proffered goblet.

A faint light emanated from the liquid sloshing against the sides. But this chalice held not wine, mead, nor ale, instead an icy flame burned within.

The Winter Queen smiled and mimicked touching an imaginary goblet to her frost-rimed lips. Exhausted beyond endurance, your smile was weak, and—not glancing at Fianait— you drank the icy liquid down.

Gasping, Fianait rushed to your side as writhing pain spread outward from your core, igniting smaller fires as it travelled through your body. Where that icy flame had touched, the fire burned the skin to welts and blisters. Uttering a final broken sob, you fell, staring up at swaying forest branches, and listening to the breathless rattle in your lungs. Time and reason abandoned you, Fianait holding you in her arms on the forest floor, huddled and twitching. Finally, you opened your eyes, meeting the violet gaze of the woman you loved, trying to speak, to offer her comfort, but nothing came from your scarred throat.

Those three tasks might have broken the strength of your mortal body, crippled your harpist's hands and stolen your minstrel's voice, but when the Sidhe Lord and his Queen departed, Fianait remained beside you, cradled in your arms.

When dawn broke among the ferns and moss, her voice sung alone in the morning.

About the Author:

Leanbh Pearson lives in Canberra, Australia. A dark fiction author inspired by mythology, folklore, archaeology, history, and the environment, her short fiction features in anthologies from international publishers. Partially fictional, she is a keen nature and wildlife photographer, bookshop, and Museum devotee, enjoying the Australian wilderness with her dogs (the canine assistants). Leanbh's alter-ego is an academic in archaeology and prehistory.

Alice's Hope

Jade Wildy

I dedicate this story to my mother, Jo Benger, who passed away from cancer in 2019.

#

Alice rolled the aged canvas into a tight coil, taking care not to cause damage and placed it into the carrier tube that kept it safe. For the hundredth time, she gritted her teeth and cursed that such a beautiful painting was hidden away in a tube carried by a 'rebel' rather than stretched on a frame and hung on a wall, but they needed it.

She coughed and flipped a finger at the twin suns that were both now high in the desert sky. The air felt like it was pulling the moisture right out of her skin as she uncapped her canteen and took a precious sip, then stowed it in her pack. She let the dry sand trickle through her fingers and wondered what grass would feel like in her hand.

Her comwatch chirped that the transmission she had been waiting on was incoming.

"Here."

"And where exactly be here?" The gruff accented voice on the other end told her it was McFae.

"Out on the mesa . . . somewhere." Alice swept her hand out towards the plateaus of bare rock and shifting sands, even though he couldn't see them. She propped her head upon her other hand. Holding it up almost seemed too much effort when every inch of her body ached, and she had to make a conscious effort to unclench her jaw. *Stop asking questions and just come get me,* she thought to herself.

"So you did survive the Capitol. Tell me, Alice, do ye have it?" McFae's voice betrayed a hint of worry.

"Yes. I have it." Alice laid her hand on the tube in her lap.

"We will send a pick-up once we have pinpointed yer location." The transmission clicked off.

Well done, Alice. Are you ok, Alice? Are you dying from your injuries as we speak, Alice? She shook her head and checked the bandage on her shoulder. Her salvaged combat suit had protected her from the worst of the firefight but made checking the bits it hadn't covered difficult. Her bandage was holding but would need to be replaced before too long. She felt along her hairline. It was sticky in places where she had been peppered with flying shrapnel and her jaw hurt where a shot came so close to killing her it had severed the strap on her helmet. That thought brought the thunder of the guns and the pain of impacts back to her. Pushing the thought away, she tried to still the tremor in her hands.

Your life isn't any more important than anyone else's, she told herself and scrunched her eyes up in an attempt to block everything out. *You have the painting, which means years of careful planning haven't been wasted.* McFae hadn't mentioned any of the others.

"Did anyone else survive?" She asked the twin suns, shaking her head. She only knew a few of them by name. Sandy-haired Robert, a grandmotherly-type called Grace, Paul who was more of a shadow than a person, and that bitchy snob, Candice. They all had the same mission—to get the painting—but each had a different plan. If one failed, there was another. The fails had stacked up until Alice. She smiled to herself and patted the tube. She had been the one to succeed.

Her comwatch chirped.

"Yes?"

"G-glad to hear your voice, Alice." Michael, their timid specialist in terraform artefacts sighed with relief.

"Not as glad as I am to have survived." She pictured his dark curls and shy side-smile.

"D-describe it." Mikey cut to the point. She liked that about him.

"Give me a moment." She pulled the carrier tube back up and unrolled the artefact. Again, she found herself surprised at its size and intricacy.

"I'm not sure how this will lead to our salvation but the painting has a tree, with a central stem and all these little curls of branches coming out—"

"What colours?"

"The tree is a mottled green, the background is shades of dark blue. There are little pictures around the outside."

"Those are the n-names of the other artefacts. They actually look like the ob-objects."

"Right. And then there are a whole lot of little symbols running all over it."

"Instructions."

"Instructions?" Alice frowned. "Mikey, what have I got here?"

"You have the s-s-schematics for the device that will bring water back to the p-planet. No more hoping the elite won't up water prices. No more being forced into the d-desert from the cities. This planet will thrive again." The excitement grew in Mikey's voice.

Alice looked out over the desert and tried to image green hills like the ones in books. "But it looks too . . . pretty to be just schematics."

Mikey chuckled. "R-rumour has it that it hung in the P-prime Leaders' bedroom for generations, but they had no idea what they had. Similar st-story for each of the artefacts."

"Why make them all so pretty?"

"There's d-different theories. I think they just didn't s-see the division of art and science that we do. All the artefacts are k-key components in the device, but all are beautiful."

Alice rolled up the painting. "When we use the artefacts, the Capitol really will lose the control they have on the planet, won't they?" She smiled to herself as she clicked the carrier tube's cap into place.

Mikey sighed. "We just need that last p-piece. And then we've got to build it."

"I guess that will be tomorrow's problem to sort out. I can hear the groundship coming. I'll see you shortly." Alice moved to cut the transmission.

"That isn't us."

She froze as cold dread trickled down her spine. "What do you mean?"

"Our ship has b-barely left. They had to t-triangulate your position. There is no way it would be there yet."

Alice swore and scrambled in her pack to find her binoculars. She spotted the ship but couldn't see any markings or crest that suggested it was a Capitol vessel. "Mikey, are you sure?"

"Alice, hide!"

She clicked off the transmission and grabbed the tube, slinging it over her shoulder, ignoring the stern protests from the injured parts of her body.

Little rocks and shale dislodged under Alice's feet, as she half ran, half slid down the rock face to finally drop into a crevasse between two plateaus, landing heavily. She stepped out of easy view under an outcrop of rock as the sound of the groundship grew near, and a shadow passed overhead. Clutching the painting close to her she flattened herself against the rock.

It had to be from the Capitol. They were closer and would have been able to get a fix on her signal sooner than the rebel base deep underground, as well as travel a shorter distance.

"Alice?" McFae's voice drifted to her from the plateau above. She held her breath. "Alice, we've come to collect ye! Let's get that artefact where it belongs."

Maybe McFae had already been on his way, and this was her ticket out. Their organisation wasn't just at one base; there were people spread out all over the planet. But Mikey said their ship had just left. She shook her head. No chance. She had to accept that despite his years of service, McFae wasn't on their side.

"Come on, girl. Don't be shy." The sound of his gritted teeth betrayed his impatience.

Heavy footsteps sounded on the rock above. Not a combat suit like hers, that was the sound of a mech suit. Only the capitol had Mech suits. Armoured, fortified and gunned up to the teeth. She could have cried.

She slid her way along under the outcrop moving slowly to produce as little noise as possible. Sweat dripped down her brow but she was thankful for the heat—they would struggle to isolate her heat signature. If it had been night she would have been dead already.

"Recheck the location," McFae demanded. "Definitely within five jots of this point." The other voice was muffled by the mech suit. Alice continued to creep away.

"Well let's try to narrow it down."

Alice's comwatch chirped. She jumped and turned it off.

Someone was moving down the side of the plateau. Her heart hammered.

McFae dropped into the crevasse. "Now why would ye be hiding? We come to take you home." McFae's face was a mass of scars earned in resistance battles fought years before Alice was born. His grey peppered beard hid the damage to his lips but could not hide the cold disdain in his eyes. Alice backed further away.

The mech stomped around above her. Pure luck made her position inaccessible to the bulky Mech suit.

McFae crouched and inched forwards with his hands held out as if Alice was an animal about to spook.

She put her hand to her gun holster. Empty. She mentally cursed. "How long have you worked for the Capitol?" Alice spat out. "Can't you see how this will improve things for everyone?"

McFae grimaced and looked away. "Just hand over the painting." Alice realised he wasn't game enough to attack her directly. "What's wrong, McFae? Not brave enough to just come take it?"

"I have *years* of experience on ye, girl."

"And every one of them shows." Neither of them was sure who would win in a fight, but if the Mech figured out how to get at her, McFae would have the advantage.

Alice continued to edge away along the rock face until her hand encountered open air.

"Give it to me NOW!" McFae's eyes flickered to the side of her and widened. It was all the suggestion she needed.

She turned and bolted into the opening, McFae hot on her heels.

The cave descended into darkness as she ran. She paused, listening for pursuit. Her heart hammered and she struggled to avoid breathing loudly. At first, she didn't hear anything. Then the cave filled with a deafening, echoing roar. She clamped her hands over her ears. The mech. It was blasting through the rock with its cannons.

Alice ran again, keeping one hand on the smooth cave wall, and the other clamped on the precious painting in its tube. At least the noise hid the sounds of her boots as she stumbled forwards. Her comwatch tracked her movement, and she hoped it was enough to get back out.

Alice moved deeper, leaving the sounds of blasts behind her. She shivered against the cold air. Her shoulder ached and the moments of pure adrenalin were replaced by deep fatigue.

She stumbled in the dark and the carrier tube's strap slipped off her shoulder to fall to the ground. She swore, crouching down to feel around for it. *Typical to risk my neck infiltrating the Capitol, sneaking into the vaults, getting the stupid painting only to drop it into a crack.* The fear of losing the painting grew as she searched.

Deciding the risk was worth it, she flipped open her comwatch. Its faint glow illuminated her surroundings enough to locate the tube which lay against the far wall. *Make it quick, Alice.* She crept across the room, mindful of how sound might travel, and knelt to pick up the carrier tube, turning it in her hands. It wasn't damaged, and the artefact inside was intact.

Her comwatch chirped and immediately connected because the cover was already open. Alice held her breath.

"Alice? Alice it's M-Mikey. Are you dead?"

She breathed out in relief. "No Mikey, not dead . . . yet. I'm in some kind of system of tunnels under the mesa. McFae and a mech are hunting me."

Mikey swore. "Our g-groundship is coming. We won't be long. Hang in there."

Alice was about to ask how long they'd be when a slow clap echoed off the walls. She spun around. McFae had found her. She clicked the transmission off but didn't bother to close the lid and lose the light.

McFae was standing in the only way out. Alice eyed him off wondering again who might win if she tried to fight her way past him. The sounds of the mech approaching made her decision for her and she launched herself at McFae, catching his face with her fist. His head snapped back and she tried to get past but he grabbed at the carrier tube. The swinging light of her watch showed blood streaming down his face from his nose. She took another shot. He dodged and sunk his own fist into her stomach. The air was driven from her lungs and she staggered. He came at her again. His blow landed awkwardly but hit her damaged shoulder. Pain seared through her and she cried out.

"Ye can give me the painting or I can take it. It's up to—"

Alice cut him off with a kick to his knee. He dropped and she staggered past him, closing her comwatch. He roared in pain and the sounds of the mech's steps quickened. A light flickered down the corridor. Of course the mech would have lights!

"She's coming towards ye!" McFae's voice echoed off the walls.

The sound of the mech grinding against the wall as it turned sent Alice staggering back down the tunnel, towards McFae.

"Be like shooting fish in a barrel!" He laughed as he grabbed her arms. The mech brought its mini guns up.

Alice swung McFae around. The shock registered on his face as the tiny projectiles ripped through him. She dove for the floor as McFae's body dropped, and desperately searched for another way out. The only gap was between the mech's legs. She looked up. Her eyes met those of the mech soldier, cast in the blue-hued light of the suit. They widened as he registered what she could do. Mini gun expended, he lined his cannons on her. They weren't designed for quick use and needed time to charge. She surged forward, wiggling her way through the gap dragging the carrier tube with her.

The mech soldier swore a torrent of abuse at her while he wrestled with the powerful suit.

As Alice ran, she looked over her shoulder, dreading she would see fully charged cannons bearing down on her. The mech hadn't turned. It couldn't; the space was too small. It had to go forwards.

You aren't safe yet, Alice. She pushed herself past the last few drops of her reserves, following the little chirps and buzzes from her comwatch that directed her back to the surface.

The opening to the tunnels was a mess of rock and rubble where the mech had punched its way through. Alice's arms shook as she climbed to the top, finding McFae's groundship on the plateau, but she couldn't pilot it without a mech suit to interface with the controls. Ignoring it she ran to the edge of the plateau, searching for any signs of salvation.

Her comwatch chirped.

"Yes?"

"Alice, we are al-almost on you. Hang tight."

"Thanks, Mikey." Alice scanned the horizon. Her rescue was a dot in the distance but was approaching fast. The sound Alice was dreading came from behind her. The mech was climbing through the broken bits of rock and sand towards her to reclaim the artefact.

Ignoring its slow-charging cannons, the mech thundered towards her, heavy boots thumping the ground. Their groundship would arrive too late to save her, but she could jump over the edge with the artefact. The resistance would find her comwatch signal before the mech could. *Unless . . .*

Alice closed her eyes and took a breath as the hulking mech bore down on her position. She clutched the tube close to her, whispered a silent prayer and stepped to the side.

A moment of distraction. A glimpse of the mech pilots surprised expression. And the mech tumbled over the edge of the plateau.

Alice walked to the edge to watch it fall. Even if it could get up, it wouldn't be able to climb up the side. Satisfied, she took a deep breath and turned to the oncoming groundship as it stirred up a flurry of sand and rocks as it landed.

Alice limped towards the groundship, the tube containing the terraforming blueprints held tightly in her shaking hands. They were now one step closer to taking away the rich's stranglehold on basic survival and restoring water to the planet. There was now hope for the future. Alice's children would know what grass felt like in their hands.

About the Author:

Jade Wildy holds Bachelor and Masters degrees in visual arts giving her a flair for culture. She returned to writing fiction in 2020, concentrating on speculative fiction but branching out into fantasy, science fiction and horror.

Through her writing Jade addresses themes like death, psychological state and being different, and delights in slipping in the unexpected. She believes in the power of storytelling as a motivator for change, and her writing has been included in numerous publications internationally.

A self-confessed wallflower, Jade lives in South Australia on the traditional lands of the Kaurna People, and can be frequently be found writing or drawing in one of the local cafes.

www.jadewildywordsmith.com
www.facebook.com/jadewildywordsmith.

Divine Engineer

Claire Fitzpatrick

For my beloved father, Peter Joseph Fitzpatrick (25/05/67 - 29/10/20). You taught me how to ride a bike. You taught me how to fish. You showed me how to use my words. You helped me to find my voice. Enjoy your beers with grandpa. I love you.

#

Elias lived in a purple tent at the bottom of an empty swimming pool. While he didn't believe in astrology, he did believe in the importance of not being too sceptical. So, he dedicated three nights a week to mapping the constellations of the night sky, hoping to find some answers amid the great tragedy that was his life.

He liked learning new things. At twenty-nine, Elias was aware of many things—how to drive a car, how to do his taxes, how to cook a meal—though he was aware there was still a lot he did not know. His mantra was the serenity prayer. And though he accepted it as psychological snake oil, it worked for him, even if his family thought he gave little fucks for anything but himself. But what was the point in devoting time and energy to things he didn't value when he could spend more energy giving a fuck about the things he did? His friends called him 'poor little rich boy,' his on-again, off-again girlfriend called him a snob. Yet he liked to think he was waiting for something or someone. Some divine engineer who would tell him how to live.

He climbed out of the pool and laid beside it on the patchwork quilt his grandmother had made for him before her dementia diagnosis, hands behind his head as he looked up at the sparkling stars. Orion the Hunter stretched above him, the band of luminescence the combined glow of millions of dead stars. He followed the stars and outstretched his finger to outline the purple and yellow archway of stars. It seemed a lightning bolt had become trapped within the sky. Once, he'd been able to see it. But now, the light pollution of the town was so bad it obfuscated many of his beloved astrological observations. The more humanity brightened the world with man-made technologies, the more they darkened the universe.

Elias pushed himself up, climbed back into the pool, and sat on his bed. He'd filled the tent with all of his belongings and had turned it into a small apartment. It was a family-sized tent with three rooms. Several rugs carpeted the floor; posters were plastered across the walls; his mattress lay in the middle room surrounded by discarded clothing. He'd turned the tent into a veritable paradise, a haven that was his own. A few years ago, when they'd emptied the pool, his parents had bought him a generator, which he used to power his portable stove-top, his phone, and several lamps.

He picked up his phone from the old chess table and checked the time. Eleven thirty PM. Fifteen minutes until the annular eclipse would begin. It would peak at two-thirty AM and end at five forty-five. They happened every year or two, though this time the eclipse would be different, for it would be visible by two percent of the Earth's surface and would reveal a solar halo around the moon, lasting minutes. Elias had never seen such an eclipse before, for it was more visible from Asia or Africa, the last only seen from Congo-Brazzaville.

As a child, his father had encouraged his interest in astronomy and had taught him about the universe. They'd have barbecues and he and his sister would sit outside and listen to his stories. While his sister enjoyed spending time with him, she'd never been as enraptured or interested in planets and stars as he was. He'd hung on their father's every word, impressed with his knowledge and ability to tell a story infused with facts. As he grew older, Elias pursued astronomy in his own time, buying books and watching documentaries. He wanted to know all he could and to understand his place in the universe.

Preparing to lose a loved one was, in his opinion, worse than losing them in an accident. He started to see death everywhere. He became more aware of funeral homes and life insurance and even churches. After cancer had taken his father, death still lingered. Over time, he started stargazing again and rediscovered his passionate interest in the universe, and the feeling that death was watching him faded away. But then, a week after his twenty-ninth birthday, he, too, was diagnosed with cancer, and death returned. He hadn't felt sick. He hadn't felt anything was wrong. But then everything happened so fast. One day he was at home watching Star Trek feeling a little sick, the next he couldn't eat and was so tired when he wasn't having chemotherapy he was sleeping.

Elias had been given everything in life, and his parents had always taken care of him and his sister. When he needed money, they did what they could to help. When he needed advice, they listened and assisted where they could. He'd never felt they didn't love him and appreciated their encouragement and support of his interests. After his failed marriage, he'd moved home to care for his mother. She wasn't sick of anything in particular, yet her loneliness affected her as a physical ailment. And while she had a young woman visit three times a week, Elias knew she loved having him around. His own diagnosis distressed her. Parents weren't supposed to outlive their children.

Elias went over to the stack of unread mail. Most of it was from political candidates and magazine subscriptions, yet there was a thick letter he hadn't noticed. Curious, he picked it up, turned it over, and read the sender's information. It simply read *Blackwood Industries* in bold lettering. Elias frowned. He had never heard of such a corporation. Yet the front of the envelope was addressed to him in cursive handwriting. Someone had taken the time to write to him. His stomach churned uncomfortably. This could only be bad news. Who wrote to people anymore? He went over to his bed, sat down, then curiously open the letter.

Dear Elias,

I hope this letter finds you well. My name is Julian Blackwood, Director of Blackwood Industries, and I am writing to offer you my services. I send my condolences to your father – he was a former colleague of mine, and over time we became fast friends. Though you do not know me, he told me much about his family before he passed, so I hope you don't find this letter insincere. Recently, I learned of your diagnosis, and after several clinical trials, I am happy to say we are now at the stage where we are confident in our ability to assist you.

I wish to offer an alternative to chemotherapy. The laboratory of Blackwood Industries has developed a possible cure, and we are confident we can eradicate your cancer. We would like to invite you to our offices before it progresses too far.

We have created a cure whereby we would induce a coma, and then inject a drug that would cause your heart to stop. We would then operate on your body, remove your cancer, then 'resurrect' you. Any parts we cannot remove we can manage with chemotherapy.

It is understandable you may be sceptical of our services. And I want you to know that is alright. I'd like to reassure you that everything we do is to support you and save your life. If you are interested in this opportunity, I invite you to meet with me at ten am on the third of July at Blackwood Industries, located at the Yale School of Medicine. The precise building and room number are written in the letterhead.

You need not reply to this letter; if you wish to meet myself and my colleagues on the arranged date, time, and location, I will see you there. If not, I wish you all the best.

I await our formal introduction.

Kind regards,

Julian Blackwood.

Elias laid down and read the letter once again. Its contents were bizarre. *We will resurrect you.* His father had never mentioned Julian Blackwood before, and—while he was interested in science—he'd been a scaffolder for most of his life. Elias couldn't imagine an occasion they would meet or work together. Putting down the letter, pulled his phone from his pocket, and google searched *Julian Blackwood, Blackwood Industries.* In a matter of seconds, he found a photo of the man standing in a lavish office. He stood with an air of confidence, arms crossed in front of a large bookcase, thick black-rimmed glasses settled on the end of his nose, dressed in a three-piece suit with a pocket-watch and a lavender silk pocket square. Elias had never seen anyone outside period television shows wear such an outfit.

Elias frowned. Why would this man reach out to him? Sure, he had once worked with his father, but why him? They had never met and had no other connection. And how had he known about the cancer in the first place? His father requested Elias and his family keep it to themselves. In any case, he wasn't sure *how* to tell people. Elias didn't want their sympathy, nor their pity. He wanted to carry on with his life as usual, and as normal as he could until the chemo made it impossible to do so. The meeting was in three days. Elias would ask his mother in the morning. She'd know who the man was.

Elias checked the time on his phone. Half an hour until the eclipse peaked. His stomach churned in anticipation. Pocketing his phone, he went outside, climbed out of the pool, and resumed his position on the quilt, head resting on his hands. Astronomers had—so far—discovered more than two thousand and five hundred stars with planets orbiting in their galaxy. The James Webb Space Telescope was scheduled to launch next year and would observe exoplanets within discovered solar systems in order to reveal more details about the distant worlds. He wondered—if there were other life in the universe—had they found a cure for cancer? Did they know how to contact Earth to share this information? And if they already had, why hadn't scientists shared the information?

Elias looked up at the sky. The sun had begun to rise, casting a pale light across the fading stars. Not long until the eclipse. Elias could have gotten in a few hours of sleep, yet his excitement kept him awake and alert. If only his father was laying beside him. There were so many things the man would miss out on. Birthdays, anniversaries, holidays. Everything.

He thought of the strange letter once again. Perhaps Julian Blackwood was some kind of mad Frankenstein-esque scientist who believed he could resurrect the dead. The idea was ludicrous. Elias had read in magazines about scientists revitalising pig brains four hours after their death. And though they said there was no evidence of awareness or consciousness, the authors concluded revitalised brain were active. Elias didn't understand it all. Surely they were the fantasies of mad scientists. He looked up at the plethora of stars and bit his bottom lip. But what did he have to lose?

Elias looked at his phone once again. Fifteen minutes. The sun rose until the full disc burned in the sky. After half an hour, the moon came into view, and consumed it altogether, leaving a small circle of light, the diamond ring. Elias held his breath as the moon moved off the sun, and the first light of the photosphere shone through, creating a necklace-like effect. He let out his breath. The sun re-emerged in a burst of light, the moon revealed more of the sun, and the corona faded from view. He stood in awe as the outer edge of the moon touched the sun once last time, and the eclipse ended. Elias looked down at his phone and gasped. Almost two and a half hours had passed since the first contact, yet it seemed to be over in a matter of minutes.

His stomach knotted uncomfortably. His dad would be so excited right now. He wondered if life on other planets witnessed such an occurrence. A few years ago, scientists in America had discovered a strange world with two suns in the sky. They called the planet HD 131399Ab, and for half of the planet's orbit – around five hundred and fifty Earth years, three stars were visible in the sky, and each day had a triples sunrise and sunset. The planet would be in near-constant daylight for around one hundred and forty Earth years. What would an eclipse look like to inhabitants on that planet? How would they react to darkness? How would they feel seeing stars for the first time? He thought of his meeting with Julian Blackwood. What if aliens from such a planet contacted Earth, with Julian, and provided him with such technology to cure cancer? The thought was ridiculous, but Elias had to have faith, for without faith there was no hope. The way to have hope was to believe in the capability of a better future. He wanted to believe Julian was not just another cog in the wheel of 'big pharma'. Sure, his own emotions about his father and himself controlled his hope, but the logical part of him knew that even if it wasn't probable, there was a *possibility* of a cure. And that was enough for him.

The golden sunrise illuminated the light blue sky as though it was igniting a candle. Mellow orange and pinks blurred together, its hue covering the sky. The light was a beacon, welcoming a new day. His mother would soon awaken and call him in for breakfast. Later, her support worker would arrive, and they'd go out shopping together, and she would buy useless things to fill the void of her unhappiness. She never mentioned the word 'cancer.'

Yawning, Elias returned to his bed and pulled the blanket up over his head. He looked around the room and grinned. Nobody believed he lived in a tent at the bottom of a swimming pool, and why should they? It was, like many of his ideas, ridiculous. Both he and his mother weren't strong swimmers, and his sister didn't visit often, so there was no need for a functioning pool. Elias closed his eyes. The two women were fiercely independent and had pursued high-paying careers. However, he was different. After university, he had worked on and off but wasn't sure what his purpose was. All he wanted to do was look at the stars. But seeing the eclipse brought him unexpected hope. For the first time since his father passed, he was determined to find a pathway. Perhaps meeting the mysterious man would steer him in the right direction?

DIVINE ENGINEER

Elias climbed out of bed and scheduled the date in his calendar. Julian Blackwood had become his divine engineer. Though his father was catholic and wore a gold cross on a necklace, Elias didn't believe in God—but he had to believe in something. He didn't want to be the poor little rich boy. He wanted to be a hopeful man who happened to want for nothing. For the first time in what felt like forever, Elias gave a fuck about trying to find a purpose. He gave a fuck about surviving. And that was all the hope he needed.

About the Author:

Claire Fitzpatrick is an editor and award-winning author of speculative fiction and non-fiction. She won the 2017 Rocky Wood Award for Non-Fiction and Criticism. Called 'Australia's Queen Of Body Horror' and 'Australia's Body Horror Specialist,' she enjoys writing about anatomy and the darker side of humanity. Her collection Metamorphosis *from IFWG Publishing was hailed as 'simply heroic.'*

She lives with her partner, an artist, and their weird goblin kids somewhere in Queensland.

Visit her at www.clairefitzpatrick.net.

Spirit of the Koi

Lisa Rodrigues

Dedicated to my father, Kenneth Rodrigues, who gave me enthusiastic encouragement for no good reason. He died of pancreatic cancer in 2020.

#

The fish feed breaks the surface. For a second, the pellets I've thrown are tiny meteors crash-landing on an unsuspecting planet, circular waves marking their impact. Then golden fins and greedy mouths flash from the deep and devour the intruders, before disappearing into the blackness of the water below.

I turn to Yen but all I see is a curtain of black hair aimed at the dark water below.

We're leaning over the edge of a red bridge in the middle of the Japanese ornamental gardens, an incongruous ode to Asia in the middle of the Perth suburbs.

"Do you know why wolves howl at the moon?" Yen asks.

She likes to tell stories. I thought she would tell me a story about the gardens—that the bridge has strong spiritual connotations, that the koi fish is a symbol of navigating the suffering of life. Any other day I would have teased her for being arbitrary by bringing up wolves. But it's not any other day, and I'm just glad she's speaking. She hasn't spoken since the funeral.

"Tell me," I say, throwing more feed into the pond.

"Wolves howl at the moon because it reminds them of home."

"Wolves come from the moon?" I ask. I smile at her but she doesn't turn. "Tell me."

She pauses, and I wait. She tucks her hair behind the ear closest to me. Her eyes are still red, although I never saw the tears spill. "The wolves are not from the moon. Their planet is very different, but the moon looks the same. Sometimes they forget they're far away, and when they remember, they howl because they miss home."

"That's sad."

"Yes."

My arms itch to wrap around her, but her eyes are distant. I want to ask—Is she the wolf? Is the wolf her brother, Matt? To ask how she feels, and how it felt to find his body. But those questions are selfish today—maybe they'll always be selfish. So instead I sprinkle more feed in the water and let her tell her story.

"So . . . space wolves?"

She doesn't acknowledge my mocking tone, but frowns as she continues. "It's not all wolves. They came to Earth because their planet was destroyed by war. They came in secret, so they took the form of local animals. Most of them chose to be human."

"Apex predator," I murmur. The koi wrestle below as if in agreement. A white one with orange and black splotches is the largest and most aggressive.

"It was the logical choice," she agrees. "But being human doesn't agree with everyone."

"No, it doesn't," I say, thinking of Matt. The funeral was small and brief. I wasn't surprised to be invited—we'd become close in a few short months—but I was surprised that there was no other family.

"The war, and the journey, left scars that were too deep to erase. Forms like wolves—with their simple minds—make life easier to bear. Humanity is . . ." she sighs.

"Complicated," I finish.

We fall silent again. The pond below is still. I hand her the bag. She takes it without meeting my eye.

"So why wolves?" I ask, leaning my weight onto the bridge.

"They were the closest to their true form and social structure. Not everyone chose wolves. The trauma for some needed an even simpler life." She drops more feed into the water and we both watch the fish twist below. "Did you know koi are a symbol of overcoming adversity?"

I'm about to tell her that yes, I did know that, but stop when I see she's looking at me for the first time all day. Her dark eyes are welling with tears. Before I can reach out to hold her she steps forward and takes my face in her hands and kisses me. Her lips are soft, and she tastes like the peppermints we ate in the car on the way here. We've never kissed before. I can't say I haven't thought about it, but I feel a pang of guilt that I'm taking advantage of her grief.

She pulls away first. "Thank you for making humanity worth it for a while." Then she steps back and throws the bag of feed past me into the pond. It sprays an arc of feed through the air before it plops down into the depths. The water erupts in a flurry of activity, and when I turn back she's gone.

The park around us is empty.

Does she regret the kiss? And what did she mean 'for a while?'

It's then that I see her phone on the ground beside us.

While I'm reaching for it, a large black koi I've never seen before jumps an arc straight out of the water as if to say goodbye.

About the Author:

Lisa Rodrigues is an Eurasian writer in her 30-somethings based in Perth, Western Australia (Whadjuk Noongar land). She was published for the first time in 2019, and in 2020 won the KSP Writer's Centre 'Spooky stories' competition and was a finalist in Writing WA's 'Flashing the cover' competition. Her natural environment used to be goth clubs, but these days she's more likely found doing acrobatics by the beach.

LISA RODRIGUES

Valuer of Souls

Kaybee Pearson

Dedicated to Gladys Pearson, my Puerto Rican stepmom; a small, feisty woman with a heart big enough to embrace her own family and us add-ons with equal love.

#

I reach for the monitor and tap the touchscreen of my fate, without hesitation, firm and resolute. Checking a psycho-biological display for a stress reaction, I expect to find excitement. *No.* Interesting. The emotion I read is satisfaction for a job well done.

Technology obeys my command, of course. With clinical precision, I observe the ice-blue cryogenic drug of eternal promise snake its way down a polyurethane I.V. catheter towards organic flesh and blood. It enters my aged vein, mingles with a greenish-purple pulse, encouraging a pumping heart to slow but not weaken.

Human flesh is weak. My spirit is willing to be invincible.

I'm laid to rest in a custom-made titanium casket-shaped carrier lined with top-of-the-range NASA-quality padding. It gleams pristine white like heaven. I imagine myself an angel with wings about to fly off into the clouds.

This is how I leave Earth: in a long sleep, a deep forgetting, a fitting end to a lifetime's ambitious dream. A body preserved in a sterile, anti-microbial cocoon, an ironic symbol of Nature's promise of rebirth—purchased with a life savings account and cashed in bonds.

My children asked why I'm leaving our world to die. *The logic of progress*, I explained. Everything has an assigned value. Economically, it is in my best interests. At this final hour, they must learn a universal truth: everything decays into worthlessness.

Even souls, my wife had shouted in my face.

I am an adventurer in search of growth and progress. It is essential to uphold the legacy of man's shiny advancement. Be proud of your husband, one of the lucky few afforded this opportunity, a race to the top.

Work hard—no regrets. Now is not the time to dwell. My mind must not inhabit memories of this passing life; missed opportunities, mistakes, losses. Not at the culmination of my life's work, when I have succeeded beyond all others.

This is how it feels to be free.

VALUER OF SOULS

My thinking slows to medicated softness, blurring any sharp edges of remorse. Shallow breaths dry in my mouth, a refusal to taste the memory of a wife's caustic bitterness. Shadows of lethargy pull me under.

Time is short and I will soon exit this world. My sedated mind imagines a window through which I wave goodbye to all I loved . . . what did I love?

I didn't love this place.

My wife refused to come with me. *How could you want to leave?* she'd cried. *Our bodies consist more of bacteria than human cells which proves we are aggregates, inseparable, connected to each other and all living things. To sever that connection is the real death.*

She possessed a primeval notion of Earth as paradise. A world shared with plants, animals, germ-ridden beasts, slaves to an eco-system.

My wife was a sentimental fool. She never understood how the game is played. Survival proves superiority; the fittest are the most valued. She couldn't accept I've come out on top. I am worth it. This is my reward.

She'll stay rooted to the soil of home. They'll bury her bones to crumble into dust, ashes to ashes, dust to dust, mixing, merging, her remains pulled under by the gravity of earth. Returning to dirt.

Where she belongs.

My sluggish brain diffuses further memories. She will not spoil my future. Regret for love relinquished is vulnerability; I cannot afford to indulge. I remain guilt-free of severed connections. Mourning will kill you. I persist, stoic, strong, my destiny sustained. My soul is like the blackest coal under the most intense pressure plunging headlong into the unknown. I'm a true believer seeking diamond-bright resurrection.

The drug has reached my eyelids, pulling them towards sleep like sinkers on a line. Sparks flicker and fracture my vision. Lights dim. Objects outside my compartment fade into black and white outlines. It is almost time. The countdown begins. I'm not ready to submerge into the finality of peace without one final indulgence before embarking on this evolutionary sojourn.

Historians tell us early humans walked the Earth as nomads. Never settling and putting down roots of belonging, no loyalty to a place called *home.* This spirit of searching, exploring, longing to discover new horizons—wishing beyond the stars—is an inherent birthright.

My ancestors, convicts, were guilty of economic crimes (*theirs of poverty, mine of wealth* according to my wife*)* and transported across a vast ocean of nothingness to unknown lands, a new world, arriving in a lucky country.

I evolved from wanderers; people leaving the insecurity of a tarnished world, caught in a vacuum of a blank slate, on a voyage to re-form scattered pieces of their souls. Wishing upon the stars.

VALUER OF SOULS

Restlessness had been passed down in my genes from the beginning of Time.

Physicists say existence arose from the Big Bang. It required an explosion to destroy the dark heart of nothingness. A massive detonation of shattering light created the stars. These stars exploded again into clouds of atoms that formed the elements, the building blocks of distant planets and life.

So, you see. We come from the stars. Our origins are star dust.

I am an explorer following in the footsteps of my ancestors. My plan is simple enough: return to the stars.

A right of passage.

Unlike my wife, I am not destined for a rooted burial. I am eternal. I am a star.

Faint musings float across my waning perception. I will not sleep forever. My entrepreneurial soul will revive in another epoch; unspoiled, absolved, reborn in a fresh realm of immaculate resources, primed and ready for work.

Alone in these last few minutes before submerging into the longest sleep of flight, my heart muscle spasms before its final freezing. The monitor displays pride, a purchase of hard-earned gain.

And now I soar, a rocket on fire in a blast of incinerating heat, escaping an emptied husk, once useful, now valueless: a dying Earth.

What a pity my family refused to witness this victory, a life support compartment on this Virgin spacecraft—my cradle of success—rocketing into space.

An explosion shoots my pod into the void with a fuelled conflagration of light. This is my personal *big bang*, enlivening the depths of my soul.

And a legacy to my children: a glorious expression of hope amidst a frozen emptiness, copying an ancestral blueprint to once again fashion new domains in Man's own image.

Renewable life is born from destruction. This is a natural evolutionary progression of superiority. It was our nature to burn our home; we came from burning stars. It requires death, a big bang, to create something from nothing. This is the law of the Universe.

About the Author:

A recovering victim of breast cancer (thirteen years and counting). When diagnosed, defied advice on positive thinking and calm abiding, instead choosing abject terror and stress eating. Luckily, a good cook and baby Buddhist (loads of self-compassion). Relies on a life rich in human dramas to write stories, a full time occupation. Shares a property in rural Tasmania (Tyerrernotepanner, Panninher and Leterramairrener country) with feral and native creatures including her small family and a scruffy poodle named Bailey.

You Better Not be Couriering Coriander

Brianna Bullen

#

Lhaera put her Ponte shoes on, threaded a ribbon through her hair, and kissed her beloved turtleian-camel Bowser goodbye. Well, she had kissed him on the nose and turned him around to go back to the Broken Star County township. She would not be needing him for this portion of her journey. Would not force the creature through the realm of the spirits, for while Bowser was hardy, he was also slow, and you needed to have your quickest wits about you to fly through that particular ghost-clogged sky.

She slapped extra liquid armour on her shoulders, rubbing it down her arms until it solidified into diamond-solid protection. The matter shifted up, forming jutting spikes around her shoulders to prevent swooping predators getting purchase.

The liquid armour slid down her hands to form gauntlets. Infused with nanobots, the material shifted, continued to run down her back and to the base of her wings. The technology was smart enough not to weigh down the delicate chitin.

Shimmering like an oil slick through the sky, she sped through the air, avoiding the eager hands of Fae and Elves who had been lost to the realm and now sought revenge. These echoes of deceased creatures were sticky and entrapping as spider-webs, composed of the same elements, every line drawn harsh. One fae-ghost with pointed eyebrows grabbed her by the ponytail, its filaments tangling through. Crying out with alarm, she forced herself not to grapple with her assailant. Instead, she concentrated on her hands, channelling the gauntlets to form into blades. She cut off her hair before the filaments embedded themselves within her skull and kept flying, not looking back.

Her Ponte shoes, coated with extra-dimensional toxins, sliced through the necks of approaching sheet ghosts who had been in the realm for so long they had lost their form and moved instead like jellyfish through the oceanic sky. The air was thick here. Electrified and weighted. It made it hard for anyone with physicality to fly through. But she was the strongest cargo-flier in the regiment and had been appointed for the trip.

Some out-of-town hero should have volunteered to take her place for the social currency, but they hadn't. So damnit, she had to be a hero. Lhaera would rather be sitting at home with a trifle bowl of grapes and her favourite trashy-giant-with-fairy bodice-ripper than out in the cold mountain air ducking past beings that wanted to kill her. There was a reason she had flunked out of hero school in the first six months. Too much pressure. Damn her mentor Phipe the Great for having faith in her. Damn her own moral compass for being fixedly attached around her neck and pointing to the required direction. Logic and her heart told her she had to do it. She just wasn't sure she could.

It was a lot of pressure. She had taken several months off from her flight battalion—with medically-approved leave—before the Andromeda flu had hit neighbouring townships with a high fatality rate. It was poor timing, really. She had been dipping her toes back into her regular position when the deaths started rolling in and the new virus containment taskforce set up, immediately subsuming her old division into a new role.

Despite being a strong flyer, and her marks with flying keeping her in the team, Lhaera at present felt that all she was good at was avoiding responsibilities and pesky ghosts. She weaved between the grabbing creatures with ease, feet not even grazing the ground as they flew close to the desert floor. A parade of sheet ghosts dived at her from the front in a successive row, but she evaded to the side, narrowly missing crashing cheek first into a sand-dune. The ghosts crashed into the sand, disappearing and then reappearing in streams from above. Their faces were gaunt and distorted, their jaws unhinged as if to eat her and their eyes were dead-cruel spider's egg-sacs deep-set in their skulls. If she could just make it to the Ilandre city border—

Ghosts didn't have a permit to haunt that far.

Lhaera could see it now, the obnoxious 'You are now leaving the Spirit Realm, please enjoy your trip and don't forget to buy a gift bag' sign up ahead. She sped up, wings clicking overtime to push her over the line. The ghosts didn't let up until the very end, one nasty gnarled spirit finger daring to graze at the cross on her medic satchel. She pulled it away as she jerked into Ilandre, the weight of the bag against her and her distracted concentration causing her to collide with a skyscraper.

She was saved from becoming a fairy-splatter by the protective barrier put up around the building to prevent such instances after one tragic incident among child pixies playing tag. It cushioned her impact and deposited her safely on the ground in a freezing green light bauble.

People stared at her through their company's windows as she experienced the downward levitation of shame. The city was notorious for its business-minded fairies, and each wore a three-piece suit with modest, lace wing coverings. They each gave her a disappointed look and head shake, jowls seeming to move in unison from their positions at their desks. She could only really see two floors of these business fairies, but it was uncanny how identical each moved and behaved. As if it were mandate to look down on couriers and every worker outside of the business. She gave them a sheepish smile in turn, a bit disappointed that the high-flyers of society didn't actually do much flying.

Well, with a highly contagious virus going on, any stranger flying through was met with suspicion, and the workers themselves were reduced to hovering in their offices permanently, with food delivered on the hour. But Lhaera hated acknowledging these impacts to life. Things were simpler for her psyche when she could pretend they were all just a bunch of snobs.

Unbeknownst to Lhaera at the time, due to her mistaken belief the immigration and traffic departments had been informed of her couriering mission by her department, she was promptly arrested. To Lhaera, the town's deputy was giving her wings a break by signalling for her to come into his giant kettle-shaped carriage. Free transport, she had thought. He had put his hand around her armoured shoulders, steering her passed the vehicle's steed. It was a Scottish Kelpie, the shape-shifting water-horse species chosen for policework for its ability to shrink down to fae level and manoeuvre through both land and water for high-speed pursuits. The drenched creature was chowing down on a mouse as Lhaera walked past. It spat the tail of one at her feet. The deputy tutted at the murderous horse. "Now Dany, that's just impolite. No swimming time for you."

The horse trotted through the township, sulking all the while. The cityscape gave way to smaller, traditional fairy cottages and markets. Lhaera leaned out of the window of the police wagon to swipe a free jam sample as they passed through the rows of colourful pop-ups while waiting at the lights. The Deputy looked at her with alarm, before handing her a slice of wonder-bread he himself had pilfered.

"I don't think that was a free sample, sir," she said, clinking her jam-jar against his can of BearHair beer between the grates separating driver from the escorted.

"Wonder-bread is a weed here. Free to a good home."

Dany the Kelpie took the lead with a teenage-moody shake of his head as the deputy took his hands from the reins to spread jam on his bread via finger-painting.

Lhaera grimaced at the globs. "Thanks for the police escort."

"Escort? We're on the way to the station for your illegal flying through prohibited airspace. Ilande is a no-fly zone in domestic areas, criminal."

Her blood pressure dropped. "Were you not contacted? Neither by your local council or the Crown?"

"The Crown, you say?" He lifted his beer with his hair to take a sip. "You're on a Crown-approved special mission? You?" His pointy nose wrinkled. "Your hair is scrappy and not even regulation, rebel. No Crown would choose someone essentially missing a limb."

"I had to cut it off." It was considered improper to have short hair as a Fae, as the hair itself was considered an essential organ for navigating high society, capable of holding up utensils when eating and communicating intent and history through braids and ornamentation. But there was no time for such sentimentality when lives were at stake. "You'll find it within the dunes of the Spirit Realm. Hair has nothing to do with my capacity to fly. My name is Corporal Lhaera, Scouting and Delivery. We're a bit stretched thin at the moment. Surely you've encountered some of my colleagues coming through with other doses?"

He signalled for Dany to stop, the Kelpie pulling up with a whinny. His beer deposited back beside him, Lhaera could see the shape of his hair now and it looked distractingly like a perfect Bell Curve. "You shouldn't be flying over the Spirit Realm. That's a class 36b misdemeanour."

"I have a permit though—" she patted down her front, but the armour was still covering up her pockets. "Although I can't really give it to you right this second. But it's urgent. I can show you what I'm couriering—"

"Hands in front of you please. No reaching where I can't see them."

115

"You were fine with me reaching for the jam—" she shut up when she saw his raised eyebrow. "Sir I have no weapons, just medicine in my bag. Which is why it's so urgent. You know, the whole Andromeda flu, right? Freezes the wings and then creeps right into the central nervous system. I have one of the first batches of the cure in my satchel. Emergency doctor-ordered flight."

"And let me guess, your doctor's pass is also covered up under all that armour?"

"Yes. I'm just a simple delivery fae."

"Hm. Sounds like illegal drug trafficking to me," he said, writing down more charges, his hair wrapped around the pencil, his actual hands on the steering wheel.

Why did she have to get stuck with some ancient officer hellbent on procedure and running around like everything was normal? Ilandre and Flisover were hit hard, and Flisover was the epicentre of it all. Could he not see the boarded up doors? The lack of activity in the street? There was a dead milkman lying beside one of the apartment complexes, clearly having dropped dropping off a delivery of food and beverages, wings frozen stiff and veins prominent along the face. She had heard they picked up the bodies in four-hour intervals in a cart similar to the one she was now in. It was eerie, how otherwise silent and clear the streets were. Everyone but selective couriers unable to navigate the streets. Even with these restrictions, the milkman had been infected somewhere along the line. It was why it was so urgent, really. Getting these vials to the hospital was vital.

"If you would just check my bag—"

"It will be checked when we get to the station. Where you will give it straight to the toxicologist."

"Please." She hit her head against the inside of the carriage. "They're necessary anti-toxins newly manufactured. If you checked your emails you should have known I was coming through. This is wasting precious, precious time." She didn't want to be so upset. Blubbering was for whales, not fairies.

"Well if your story checks out you can go on your way, but I smell a rat."

She glared at him through the grates before her eyes widened. "Pig."

He tutted. "Just reeling in the misdemeanours aren't you, you disrespectful little wenc—"

His complaints were cut off under the bone-breaking crunch of his Bell-curve head becoming a nearly straight x-axis. Any scream was quickly muffled under the mouth of the flying boar.

Dany swore, sensing his partner's demise. "Fuck this shit, I want to live." The laconic sheriff kelpie sped off, catching the head of the snuffling killer in the window between prisoner and driver.

117

Lhaera screamed and dived back, away from the bloody-mouthed, tusked creature. The pig chewed at the air, gnashing its teeth and snorted around. It squealed, either delayed from the pain or angry that it couldn't reach her. Rabid eyes, usually unseen due to layers of skin-flaps were visible from this close, pulled back by the frame. Lhaera stared up into the bloodshot eyes of the truffle-pig, aware that it was trained to eat both the remainder of her hair (with the head attached) and her wings.

They were supposed to have been decommissioned following the elf-fairy war of '86, but wild strays had been known to fly freely. The elves didn't seem to care too much. If they weren't part of their command, and weren't bred to kill elves, they weren't their problem. The pig's forked, stainless steel hooves were scraping against Dany's neck as it tried to shove itself further in with an unruly shriek.

In sudden agony, Dany rammed the side of the carriage into the nearest building, trying to break the creature's neck. It dislodged its head from the frame. The impact shattered the cart and Lhaera also went tumbling out. Dany ran free, experiencing freedom from the weight on his back for the first time in twenty years. He whinnied victoriously. He had some enemies to drown.

Lhaera lay on the pavement face-first, silver blood dripping from her forehead. Dazed, possibly concussed, she groaned as she came back to consciousness. Slowly, engulfed by pain and stars, she rose onto her hands and knees and staggered up. She glanced behind her, the flying pig squealed and wriggled wildly from its position sandwiched between building and cart. There was a tear in her lower wing the size of a penny. In time it would scar over, but for now, there was the risk of future spread. Her aching wings would have to hold her. She looked back at the tatters and winced, but the thrashing of the boar gave her the adrenaline needed to keep going.

The ride through town had brought her closer to the hospital. Incompetence could occasionally save the day. The pig was now free and staggering to its stainless feet. Her wings fluttered overtime and she pulled her satchel close, feeling it for any breaks and dampness from the crash. The bubble-wrap lining the bag and vials had clearly done their work. She was about to cross into a protective circle of flowers and mushrooms—a marked fairy circle—when the grunting pig lunged and took a bite out of her lower wing. Lhaera screamed and veered sideways, pulled in part by the pig as it collapsed to the ground with a dying sigh. The remains of her left wing fell out of its slackening maw.

She got out from under the pig, weighed down though she was with her applied armour, and stood in shock on her tiptoes, just willing herself to move before the adrenaline wore off and the pain set in. She couldn't help herself from looking back and winced, the pain in her tattered wing now throbbing. The blood in her wings was darker silver, almost black. It dribbled onto the ground like a Rorschach ink-stain.

She tip-toed for about a mile before her feet were close to giving up, the infinitesimal progress and sheer body weight on her ill-formed feet caused her to scream in frustration, and a feral turtleian-camel fell into the pool it was drinking from in surprise before it swam away in the water below. The motion was hurried and fluid, a complete contrast to her sweet Bowser's clumsy swim strokes. No people were on the path and there were only a few vehicles. Most were tending to family struck down with the virus, or in self-imposed lock down.

When the pain in her feet got too much she switched to flying; when the pain in her one-and-a-third wings got too much she switched back to walking. Every nerve and muscle screamed in agony, but what else could a courier do?

When she got to the Hospital, the gates unlocked themselves and the doors swung open. There was not much fanfare. Just a rushed 'thank god' and the removal of her satchel by someone she had to hope was a doctor. Some nurses came to either side of her, ferrying her to a bed still cold from the body that had just been carted away. She groaned, letting out her wounded pain because she was finally in a comfortable space, cared for, and able to do it.

Her head was jerked up as they fluffed up her pillow, made with the down of baby dragon feathers, as the nurses administered the IV containing her carried medicine. The sap-orange fluid went slowly into the ghost-pale and shuddering child to her right. Their shivers gradually subsided as the colour returned to their mouth and face, lips no longer blue. The veins in their wings, previously a steely silver, dilated and flooded with near-black colour. The chitin scales defrosted, the green no longer sickly but deep emerald. Their eyes, frozen over and unfocused, now locked with hers and smiled. They sighed contentedly and got comfortable on their own pillow

"Oh no you don't," the nurse on hand said, unwrapping her from her blanket. "There are other sick people in the corridor, piss off."

They looked like they wanted to argue, but used their new-found strength to fly away faster than a kid in a family of seven called down to dinner.

"That poor kid." The nurse turned to her with a sniff. "Lost her entire family, caught the virus when lining up for food stamps. She can fuck right off though."

Lhaera coughed into her fist. The armour had retracted and was now a leech line slapped across her collarbone. "Fair enough. I'll get out of your way as soon as I catch my breath—"

"Oh no, dearie," she said kindly. "You're the hero of the hour. Stay as long as you need to, you champion, you survivor you."

". . . But only for the hour?"

"Of course." Her sparkling eyes flattened. "Heroes of the hour only get their bed fees waived for the hour, then you're just as much of a nuisance as anybody else."

Lhaera let out a hearty laugh. "Of course."

"But thank you," she said. "You saved everyone."

"Well. Not everyone. Half of the medicine is placebos. Experimentation and all."

"What?"

"I'm joking." Lhaera sat up, wincing as her damaged wing partially peeled off. "Ouch. Dark humour keeps my mind off things."

"Yeah." The nurse's eyes evaluated her wing. "We're going to have to amputate."

"Yay." Lhaera grimaced.

"But we'll get you set up with a prosthetic."

"Yay." She perked up.

"It's still in its own experimental phase."

"Yay." she slumped.

"But it comes with a laser beam for targeting threats."

"Yay!"

Job well done on surviving across the perilous terrain, Lhaera slept off her pain.

Well, under the matron's rigid time-keeping, it was more like a nap.

About the Author:

Brianna Bullen is a Deakin University PhD creative writing candidate writing about memory in science fiction. She won the 2017 Apollo Bay short story competition and placed second in the 2017 Newcastle Short story competition. Her spec-poetry chapbook Unicorns with Unibrows *is currently out as part of Puncher & Wattmann's Slow Loris series.*

BRIANNA BULLEN

Way-Bread Rising

Tansy Rayner-Roberts

\#

When the city burned, we made sandwiches.

"If there's anything worse than dying, it's dying hungry," my Gammer used to say when she taught me the secrets of way-bread and spice-bread, of courage-cakes and flapjacks, and the best scone dough in four counties.

"Heroes need to eat," she added, when she caught me staring at the recruitment posters for the army, the home guard, or the fire crews. "And ordinary folks, they're heroes too, when the clouds come down. They need to know they can have something in their bellies when the worst comes to pass."

I don't think Gammer was thinking of dragons when she said 'the worst comes to pass' but maybe she was. She's lived a long time, and seen a lot of bad crud.

At first, the dragons were only rumours, and then they were distant shadows. No one believed they were coming until it was too late to cool our bricks and pretend the city was empty.

The city ordinances started rolling in, with instructions on how to get ahead of the disaster. Too little too late, the shopkeepers on our street all agreed.

Lanterns were no longer to be lit, day or night. That was the first rule. Then, ovens weren't to be fired up except in full daylight, and that changed the way we bakers did things, I can tell you.

In the early days, more people were hurt for lack of lanterns than had ever been wounded by a dragon, in our little city at least. Carriage accidents, tripping and falling, even some accidental poisonings.

Gammer and I slept late for the first time since we were babies as we weren't allowed to spark up our wood ovens until after dawn.

There were complaints. Ordinary folk who hadn't quite taken it in, that the world was changing. They wanted their bread first thing like always, but it wasn't there to buy. Plenty of folk came banging on our door after dark, expecting they could pay a penny to bake their dinner in our ovens like always.

Then the raids got worse, and the death toll rose. Actual deaths from actual dragons. There weren't so many complaints after that. Folks were glad to get bread at all, even if they had to queue until noon for the second baking batch, or the third.

Some things didn't change though, even amongst the chaos and smoke. One of those things was that Gammer baked way-bread on Clemsdays. It was the best way-bread you could buy, everyone knew that. It took four hours to prove, weighed down as it was with so many of the good spices and secrets and dried fruits that made it so tasty. But when that bread was baked with Gammer's magic touch (I know we're not supposed to say 'magic' these days, but everyone knows she learned her trade from the fair folk), somehow it came out thin and light as air, until it found its home in a soft belly, and then it hardened up so you never needed more than a bite to keep you going for a day.

If you were travelling far, a loaf of Gammer's way-bread would take you further than any other, and keep your strength and courage as high as your chin. She only made it on Clemsdays, because when jaunters and questers set out, they left straight after the temple chants of High Bundas and they'd want their bags packed the day before.

As the dragons circled nearer, people started asking for the way-bread all week 'round. Either because they were packing up to leave—more and more of our neighbours planned to escape to the mountains or the coast—or because it would make the best rations as they hid out in their cellars and cupboards, hoping the worst of the attacks would pass over their heads.

Gammer didn't gripe about the extra work. She warmed up more yeast and set about making batch after batch of the best-smelling way-bread in the business. Every now and then she tossed in a handful or two of chocolate chips when she thought the customers needed particular cheering.

With Gammer baking nothing but way-bread, it was down to me to bake everything else. And sure, I glanced at those army posters from time to time (though there wasn't much time to go around, I can tell you) but I knew what I was doing was good. Important. Necessary.

And then . . . well, you know what happened then.

* * *

It's been six days since the city burned, since the dragons made their final assault.

Gammer and me got out, though I had to pry her old hands away from the oven when the final warning sounded.

We got out with two packs full of fresh sandwiches, a few bags of flour and sugar, and as many loaves of way-bread that we could grab.

We've been feeding people on the road for days now, and our packs are getting lighter. But bread's not all we brought with us. There's Gammer and her secrets of baking, all the know-how of yeast and crumb she's learned all these years. There's me, with my quick hands and ability to follow instructions (and the even more vital skill of knowing when to ignore the instructions of your stubborn old coot of a grandmother because the whole dratted city is on fire and it's time to get *out*).

And then there's our other treasure: the sourdough starter that Gammer's been coaxing along since before I was born. She claims she had it from her mother-in-law on the day of her wedding, and there's not one person who says otherwise.

Our plan is to keep walking until we get to a place with an oven, a place where folks need from us what they've always needed from us. The comforting scent of loaves on the rise, and a promise of a full belly once the baking is done.

We're going to be all right, Gammer and me. Come and see us when we're settled. Follow the scent of our baking, and we'll find you something to eat.

About the Author:

Tansy Rayner Roberts (she/her) is a SFF writer who lives on Palawa land, in Tasmania (lutruwita). Tansy is the author of the Creature Court trilogy, the Teacup Magic novellas, and Musketeer Space, among many other titles. She also writes crime fiction under the name Livia Day.

Sign up to Tansy's newsletter for book news and tea reviews. https://tinyurl.com/tansyrr.

Bitter Brews

Kirstie Nicholson

In memory of Annie.

#

When I was an infant I was full of courage. It was easy when I did not know what I could lose.

Now I am unable to find the courage for the simple act of knocking on my parents' door. When their eyes fall on me, and they recognise their blue-skinned child, what will they do? I am braced for the gasps of surprise and dismay, for the door to be shut in my face. But the tale of my life since they left me on the mountain-side is on my tongue, ready to spill over until there are no words left. Despite my fears, the hope will not abandon me that the door will be held wide open. All I want is for them to listen.

I remember whispers above my cradle, rough hands thrusting me into the sunlight, and fingers pushing the tender points where my horns were budding. I cried out, biting the hand that supported me. There was a sharp intake of hissed breath. "Changeling," it muttered.

* * *

I looked a normal baby in my first months. When my skin turned to cornflower blue, and my eyes became flecked with gold, a doctor was called, and then a wise man. The wise man talked of curses, of demons and sprites. He frightened me. I struggled in my cradle, but what can a baby do but squall and fling its puny hands. I tried to crawl away, but two strides from my father matched me, and I was put back in my place.

"He understands us, I think," said the wise man, and they looked on me with fear.

Before they took me, my mother made them vow not to harm me. Perhaps she hoped I would be left on the doorstep of strangers who did not mind my cursed appearance. When she embraced me for the last time her hands were gentle, but she looked at me askance. I gripped her blouse with my stubby fingers, dread unravelling inside of me, but I was pulled from her and swaddled. I stared up at my father, accusing him with my yellow eyes. He shivered, but he did not stop.

They took me to the craggy slopes of the mountain, where wildcats roamed and eagles circled overhead. The wind was cold upon the peaks, and the smell of rain was in the air. My father held me at a distance as I wailed, my cries echoing among the rocks. There came a terrific thunderclap, as though the mountain was pulling up its roots. My father's hands tensed around me and I wailed all the harder, but that thunderclap was my saviour. The wise man thought it an ill omen, fearing that the unseelie creature that had spawned me would be angered by my destruction. Better not bring its wrath upon the village by dashing me upon the crag, as they had planned. So they left me just as the storm broke, with the unyielding granite as my new crib.

The world was black and cold. Rain stung my skin. I bawled, and when no-one came, I struggled and kicked until my swaddling loosened. Freed, I crawled away over the lichen-covered rock, instinct guiding me. The storm had blotted out the mountain but my senses were as keen as a wild creature's. The wind carried the green scent of herbs from one direction, from another the musky notes of animal urine. I crawled towards the herbs, familiar to me from the kitchen, my chubby legs working hard. My hands struck a small ledge. I struggled over it and ventured forward until I met icy water flowing down a worn channel in the rock. My hands flew out in front of me, my chin smacked the granite, and I was pushed by the fast-flowing water down the slick rock until, sprawling, I scraped to a stop.

The storm thundered around me. It was the loudest thing I had ever heard, like some enormous wildcat roaring at me from the sky. Lightning flashed, illuminating the crag and the forest below it. I froze. That flash had revealed a black void before me. The crag ended here, and I had been about to crawl right off it. Wavering, I wobbled on my knees as thunder rolled over me. I wanted to cry, to scream and scream until my mother picked me up in her warm embrace and held me close. Her abandonment hurt more than the scrapes on my palms and knees, or the bruise on my chin. With the cold seeping into my bones, I turned away from the ledge.

The scent of green herbs came to me again, bringing with it thoughts of my mother collecting parsley while I was swaddled to her chest, her kisses on my brow, her long fingers catching at my own grasping ones. The smell pulled me forward. The plant was growing from a crack in the stone, sheltered by a boulder. Weary and frightened, I huddled there, protected from the pummelling rain. Hot tears spilled over my inky blue cheeks until I choked on them. Then, breathing in that comforting smell, I curled up into the lee of the boulder, and fell asleep.

When I woke I thought I was in my crib. I rolled over, the bright sunshine making me blink. A gust of chill air rippled over me, and I remembered I was lost and alone. I gripped at the tufts of the weed that had saved me and gazed around with wide golden eyes.

There was a grey expanse of rock above me, thin trees to one side, and a blue sky spotted with clouds. The black silhouette of a bird circled over me, and I watched it, captivated by its shape, until the emptiness in my belly drove me to explore.

When I moved, a shadow fell over me and I blinked in surprise as my eyes met the golden orbs of a mountain cat. She was grey like the granite, with tufted black ears and paws bigger than my head. Crouching low like a boulder, so close I could feel her hot breath, she watched me as a gnat buzzed about her head. I watched her back and felt no fear. Without hesitation, I stretched my arms towards her.

There came a deep growl from the base of her throat and she moved to nip the back of my neck. Her teeth pricked like needles and I squalled. Drops of blood slipped down my neck and pattered onto the granite. I was bawling hard when two hands clamped down on me. One moment I was caught up in the she-cat's jaws; the next I was watching her leap down the crag, ears flat upon her skull.

My rescuer murmured, stroking my back with long bony fingers. I stared up, my face hot with tears, but the sun blinded me. I thought my parents had come for me, but something was wrong. This person smelled like smoke and marsh-water, and her voice was rough and cracked.

She bent to the stone and pressed a finger to the dark spots on the granite. Touching the blood to her tongue, she sang. "Blood on stone, a child forsook, Mother Crag comes to look." She crooned the words like a lullaby, but her hands were rough and she jerked me to-and-fro as she sang. Then there was a crack and a rush of air, and the mountain-side was gone.

* * *

Mother Crag raised me like a young rabbit she wanted to fatten up for roasting. Her wits were sharp as knives and she was stronger and swifter than the mountain cat she'd taken me from. She looked an old woman, with a broken back and a shroud of ashen hair, but her human form was just a skin she wore. Every time she looked at me with her black eyes, my skin crawled with fear.

She made me a bed of straw and rags in a crate. When my shrill cries went on for too long, she drew my breath from my lungs with a mutter while I gasped in sudden silence. As I grew I learned to be quiet. I made friends with the shadows in the crannies of her tumbledown hut and hid in them like a mouse.

When I could walk and my hands lost their clumsiness, Mother Crag gave me work to do. I swept the pine needles from the porch and collected kindling. I gathered wriggling insects from the pond and fed them to the rats she kept. I stirred the huge pot that sat on top of the cooking fire with a scarred wooden spoon while Mother Crag loomed over me, concocting her strange-smelling brews.

The first time she used my blood she called me to her and bid me show her my hands. Then, fast as an adder, she pricked me with a needle of sharpened bone. Blood welled on my fingertip. She seized my arms at the elbow and hefted me off the ground to the lip of her pot. I dangled over the edge and watched wet-eyed with pain as the droplets spattered into the bubbling liquid.

"No tears," she snapped, slapping them from my cheeks, "they spoil the brew."

I was not the first child she had taken from the mountain-side. In years past, villagers often left unwanted or ill-formed babes on its slopes. But I was a prize, for my blood had a special quality that enhanced her brewing. Once I asked her where the other children had gone. She grinned at me, exposing her sharp and foetid teeth, but said nothing. I waited for Mother Crag to bring another foundling home from the mountain, but she never did. As I grew older, watching her grind bones to fine dust in her mortar, with dead forest animals strung up from the beams above her, I tried to be glad. I didn't want to make anyone else suffer this with me. But still, I hoped.

Memories of my parents came to me in dreams. I clung to their phantom warmth, soaking up the feelings of happiness the visions brought me. I waited for some sign of affection from Mother Crag. Though she terrified me, she was the only parent I had. Driven by loneliness, I befriended the caged rats, the brown frogs in the pond, and the crows that continually squawked from the hut's roof. But Mother Crag watched my efforts through slitted eyes and delighted in torturing any creature I treated with affection. My heart broke more times than I can remember.

As my palms and wrists accumulated the silver lines of thin scars, I realised that to Mother Crag I was just like the wriggling centipedes she added to her mixing pot. That's when I dreamt of fleeing the gloomy hut and its dank clearing. But at the line of trees, I always halted, fear of Mother Crag's anger squirming in my belly.

* * *

Once every moon or so, Mother Crag would sell her brews at the fêtes and market days of nearby villages. She had little use for coin. The price she extracted from her customers was steeper than a handful of copper and silver. With each brew, she placed an invisible chain upon her victim that fed her their hurt and pain. The misery that her curse-laden potions wrought made her strong and fat.

The next time she packed her cart, I asked to come with her. She had no reason to refuse. I was a pair of hands to order about, and terror kept me obedient. My small frame stumbled along the uneven forest trails after her, pulling the overladen cart until my shoulders ached, while she stabbed at me with a fallen branch and warned me that the villagers would string me up in the square if I did not hide my face. Her threats made my heart beat with fear.

All evening and into the night, people found their way to Mother Crag's tent. I sat outside, hidden in the shadows. I watched the villagers sneak inside, emerging minutes later clutching vials and bottles in their fists. I knew that this was my chance to run, but I was bewildered by the noise and clamour of the fête, and frightened that the villagers would turn on me when they saw my face. I stayed where I was, feeling the hours slip by, tortured by my indecision and the prospect of returning to the hut. I was still there sometime after dusk when the sounds of revelry had ebbed, and a woman approached with her head down, casting about with wide eyes as if afraid of being recognised.

"Here to see Mother Crag?" I asked, daring myself to speak. The moonlight fell on my face as I rose to my feet, and she stepped back apace, stifling a gasp. Her reaction made my courage falter. Quickly, I stepped back into the shadows.

Her eyes lingered on me, but she stepped into the tent. Curious, I followed, guessing at what she desired from Mother Crag. I crept into a corner and listened to her whispered plea. She was childless. Would Mother Crag help her? Mother Crag fingered her bottles and vials. They clinked against each other as she selected one with her long fingers. She promised a bonny babe, an easy birth. But hidden in my corner, I knew better. A price would have to be paid. The babe would become ill or harbour some hidden defect. That was how Mother Crag's brews worked. I frowned, realisation growing in me. I looked at my hands, the colour of a cloudless sky. I felt where my horns caught at the rough fabric of my hood. Would the babe be a changeling, like me? Was that Mother Crag's trick? Had my own mother come home one day with a brew tucked deep in her apron pocket?

The woman was ready to step outside, brown glass bottle clutched to her chest.

"Wait," I cried. I sprung at her and knocked the bottle from her hands. She wailed and fled from the tent.

Behind me, Mother Crag hissed like a snake about to strike. "Your mother still weeps," she said, the woman's coins clinking in her palm. "regret tart as green berries. Sorrow like salt." She ran her tongue over her lips, smacking them in my face.

I was trembling. I felt myself break like a birch twig. I snatched at her precious vials and threw them to the ground.

"The more you smash, the more blood to catch," she warned.

I didn't stop. I unstoppered corks and poured the stinking liquid onto the trampled grass. I crunched the glass beneath my feet and strew her wreaths of herbs like chaff. She snapped her bony fingers, her mocking smile now a snarl. Flushed with temper, I threw one of the vials at her face. She shrieked in rage.

Horrified at what I'd done, I stumbled away. But she was swift, and in an instant had me by the throat, her skeletal arms unfolding to their full length. She lifted me into the air, my glass-sliced feet kicking at her waist. I wanted to cry out, but I couldn't draw breath. Was I some demon spirit switched in the womb by Mother Crag's spell? I struggled, trying to speak.

"Behave," she growled, squeezing my throat until I thought my head would burst.

I sunk my teeth into her gnarled hand.

She shrieked with delight and pulled me closer to her grizzled face. "Bite away little weasel," she crooned, and dropped me.

Air rushed back into my burning lungs. I reached out until my fingers found an unbroken vial. The liquid inside of it was dark with my blood. I seized it and struggled to my feet, the pain of a thousand needles pricking my fingers fresh in my memory.

Mother Crag muttered curses to herself, casting her eyes over the wreckage. I stared at her with a thumping heart and loosened the vial's stopper, swallowing my fear. Her gaze swept the mess of broken bottles at my bleeding feet. When her black eyes glared down at me and her worm-like lips opened with a snarl, I saw my chance. Clutching the vial, I thrust it into her mouth with all my strength.

She spluttered like a dying fish, her eyes growing wide and full of fear. Within seconds, she spat out the vial, letting it fall to the ground with the rest of the smashed glass. But it was empty.

With a roar of rage, she lunged at me and threw me aside. I crashed into the tent, pulling it down on top of me. My chest was tight with the thought of what I'd dared, and what Mother Crag would do to me when she found me. But when I thrashed free from the ragged tent, all I heard was moaning from the black shape beneath it.

I did not wait—I ran.

* * *

I feel that impulse now, to run. As I stand here at my parents' door, the memory of my abandonment fills my thoughts. It is as fresh as the wind that blows in from the ocean. It stings like salt. But despite all I have suffered, my heart is full of longing, not anger. I pull my cloak around me. The air is chill, the shadows have grown long, and still, I wait upon the threshold. Fear urges me to flee. But hope holds me.

I remember what I have overcome to be here, and feel a surge of courage. My fist is on the door, and I knock.

About the Author:

Kirstie Nicholson is a writer of fantasy and science fiction. She studied English literature at the University of Western Australia and has previously been published in The Underground zine. She enjoys reading, playing role-playing games and spending time in nature.

Chocolate Cake and Carnage

Aiki Flinthart

For my family.

#

Clare O'Malley lay on something that had vague pretensions to mattressy-ness, yawned, and read—for the hundredth time—the crude graffiti scratched into the grey concrete ceiling. This place needed a better class of criminal to liven it up.

Good thing tomorrow was cake day.

She contemplated her options, should it fail to arrive. They were limited, dubious, and could be fatal.

The best kind, in fact.

She stroked the thin skin on her wrist where her fake ID chip lay embedded. Her plan was simple; foolproof . . . in a make-it-up-as-she-went kind of way. Which was half the fun.

And with the fee from this job she could pay off her debt. The Chancer brothers' debtors often panicked, ran, and quite literally lost their heads over failing to pay on time. Her payment was just the *tiniest* bit overdue. A month, at most.

Clare nibbled on a fingernail, tearing a crescent off and spitting it onto the grimy floor. A second went the way of the first.

No. She dismissed the potential problems. The brothers must recognise her value, even if she'd never met them. Otherwise, why give her an extra two months to pay?

She spat out another fingernail, sucked a deep breath and closed her eyes. Time to get some sleep. Hopefully.

Below, her bunkmate snored in a most unladylike fashion.

Clare groaned. Again?

Her cellmate's lack of feminine graces was hardly surprising, given Clare had used a self-adhesive prosthetic penis, fake ID chip, and a false DNA sample to get into the dycerium prison-mine's male barracks. Amazing how reluctant a hetero guard was to touch another man's genitals. Lucky for her, too. And lucky her small breasts passed for man-boobs.

Well, sleep was out. May as well get ready for the morning.

She reached into her coarse, prison-grey pants and unattached the member in question, wincing when it snagged a few hairs. By the faint light of the two white moons shining through the grotty window, Clare extracted four small hypo darts from the testicles, then a plastic detonator wire, and a pair of old fashioned lockpicks from the penis' shaft—which slumped, limp and useless. She repressed a snorting laugh and tucked it back into her underwear. The picks, wire, and darts went into a pocket.

All that was missing was cake. Chocolate, preferably.

And she needed to find Iain MacDiarmid, of course.

Retrieving him might prove a little tricky. When MacDiarmid's parents had hired her to free him from Redworld's notorious dycerium mine-prison, they'd failed to mention—until after she'd signed the contract—his addiction to snorting black. That stuff turned brains to rice pudding. When the buzz wore off, addicts developed a trigger-happy attitude that lent a certain thrill to standing between them and their next fix.

Good thing MacDiarmid's parents came from the level of wealth only found in the Hegemon Alliance's Inner Systems planets. They were paying by the day. It had already taken her three weeks to track him this far.

Clare grinned.

Breaking a black addict out of prison might be . . . exciting. But the money was worth it.

And, really, she only had to get him out of a secure prison protected by elite Grey Guards, across a wide-open kill-zone, over an electrified fence, past a kennel full of tracker-dogs, through a smallish jungle of poison-tipped sentient vines, over a rather wide river, and to her sleek little flipship, the *De Lune,* currently hidden in the crater of an almost-dormant volcano.

Easy as.

It was just a matter of waiting for the cake. She yawned and her eyes drifted closed.

Her cellmate snored again, louder this time.

"Oh, for feck's sake!" she muttered.

The gargling rattle increased in volume. He'd returned from solitary, battered and bloodied, the evening she'd arrived. Then he'd ignored her for two days and she'd ignored him right back. He did have an impressive glare, though. Even if his ice-blue eyes were bloodshot and his nose a bit bent from the guards' kind attentions.

He snorfled and cried out, thrashing in his nightmares. Outside, a guard yelled an obscenity and thumped on the transparent-alzin wall separating the cell from the hall.

Sighing, Clare waited until the guard sauntered away. Then she clambered down and jabbed one of the hypo darts into her oblivious cellmate's neck. A waste of a paralytic, but better than strangling him. She'd never killed anyone . . . deliberately, anyway. But after two nights of no sleep, he was lucky she didn't stuff his own foot in his mouth—along with his arm—and possibly his head up his arse as well.

Instead, she rolled him onto his side. The snoring stopped.

Back in bed, she closed her eyes and dreamt blissfully of chocolate cake

* * *

Dawn clawed its way into the small cell far too early and far too portentously blood-coloured. But portents were for superstitious types, which Clare was not.

She repositioned the annoying putty dick—left side or right? Hmmm. Right. How did men put up with such ridiculous floppiness always getting in the way? After a quick pat of her pockets, confirming the darts, wire, and picks were still there, she leapt out of bed and rubbed her hands together.

Today was delivery day. Today MacDiarmid's parents had arranged for the rest of the escape plan to arrive. Today she'd return the prodigal son to his parents, get a hefty wad of credits and be off to a new level of naughtiness and crime.

She pressed her face to the clear wall, squinting down the hallway in search of the mail cart and the surly guard who manhandled it—or perhaps rathandled, since he was a Yasti.

Ahhh . . . there he was. All rodenty teeth, shifty black eyes, and clawed pink hands. A disruptor dangled from a well-worn hip-holster. Did he practice drawing in front of a mirror, or was it worn from real use? She shivered. No stunners on Redworld. It was obey, or die with your innards, muscles, and bones shocked into goo.

Clare grimaced. Prisons were *so* not her kind of place. Bars. Now bars were excellent. She smacked dry lips together. Right after dropping MacDiarmid home, it would be drinks all 'round.

The mail-delivery guard was taking forever. Hers was the last cell in the row so she waited with enforced patience while he painstakingly delivered small parcels or transferred electronic messages directly to wrist-chips.

The big, square, black box on the cart *had* to be the cake. Delicious irony. Oldest prison escape ruse in the books. No file inside, though. That would be useless against transparent alzin.

Now the cart was only four cells away and the box is still there. It hasn't been delivered to MacDiarmid yet. He must be close by. Excellent.

"Wh . . ." Her cellmate sagged onto his back. He rolled his eyeballs until his bleary gaze fixed on her. The paralytic hadn't completely worn off, yet. "Wha'd oo do? Fecking . . ." He managed to raise one shoulder off the mattress.

"Temporary paralysis. You were snoring." Clare patted his head. "Don't fret. You'll be fine. Give it half an hour at the most." She hesitated. "Actually, I can probably do you one favour while you can't punch me. Hold still." She pressed the heels of her hands against the bridge of his nose and squeezed.

Bone and cartilage crackled. He gargled a scream, which she muffled with a forearm.

"Shut up, moron. The broken nose makes you snore. I fixed it. Be grateful."

His eyes narrowed. "Ow. Feck you."

"No thanks. You're not my type." She pressed against the clear wall again. The mail cart was only two cells away, now. Black package still onboard. She glanced back at her cellmate.

Could it be?

His parents hadn't given her a holo image to ID him by, just a description. Muscular, blond, blue-eyed. But that fit a third of the humans in this place. And Snorey here had come in so covered in blood it was almost impossible to tell his hair colour.

The cart came closer, cake still in place.

Well, well. She smiled. Luck was really on her side. Looked like her cellmate was her target. Come to think of it, the purpling around his bloodied nostrils could be from snorting black.

He grunted and flopped on the bed like a landed flounder.

"Ah . . . crap." She wrinkled her nose. Perhaps the paralysis hadn't been such a good idea. The escape couldn't wait and nor could she. Morning routine gave her only one hour before mining started and everyone trudged into too-narrow, too-well-guarded dycerium mine tunnels.

The potentially-handy mailcart rolled up to her door.

Clare eyed the Yasti and palmed one of her three remaining darts. Could she? Not the stupidest idea she'd ever had, but close to it. Ah, well. The money was worth the risk. Hopefully.

Any second, the door lock would disengage. That was her chance.

Instead, the rodent opened the black box and eyed the contents. He reached in.

"Hey!" Clare said. "Bad idea. Not yours."

The guard's bottomless black eyes fixed on hers as a clawed hand withdrew a large, gooey slice of the richest, mooshiest-looking chocolate cake ever baked. Clare wiped her mouth. Dinner had been a long time ago.

"Whaas hapnin?" Her cellmate seemed to be regaining some control over his tongue.

"Your cake is being eaten by the guard."

One slice of cake vanished into a cavernous, betoothed maw and the Yasti patted his paunchy belly.

Well, one slice didn't matter so much. She could still get the job done. He just needed to pass the damned pastry over. She glared at the guard, who responded by lifting out a second slice.

"Ahhh, c'mon," she growled. "I need that."

He ate a third.

"Who sent the cake?" MacDiarmid asked, more clearly.

Clare watched a fourth slice disappear and sighed. This plan was so not going to plan. Feck it. "Your parents," she whispered testily. "They sent me to get you out. But fatso here—" she jerked a thumb at the guard "—is seriously disrupting things. Any more and I shall be *very* irritated."

MacDiarmid twisted his neck, craning so he could see the door. "What kind of cake, strawberry or chocolate?"

"Chocolate." Clare raised a brow. "What does it matter?"

"Feck!" He muttered a few more choice words and rolled out of bed, landing with a painful-sounding thump on the concrete. "Ow. Again." With many grunts and curses, he wormed his way underneath the bunk until all she could see was a shock of hair and one foot.

Outside, the guard showed her the empty box and tipped crumbs on the floor. Only then did he thumbprint the door lock. The mechanism clicked open.

Clare studied the Yasti's hairy throat, looking for somewhere particularly painful to jab the dart.

"Get down, you idiot," came a hiss from the shadowy corner under the bed.

"Why?" She checked the gap in the door. Almost wide enough. To keep it open, all she had to do was overpower one of the sneakiest, fastest species in the galaxy. No problem.

A hand appeared from under the bed and feebly clutched at her ankle. Ice-blue eyes peered out at her. "Because it's a fecking *chocolate* cake! How much do you like living?"

"I'm fairly keen on it, actually. But why the fuss? Your parents sent me—and the cake. Are you allergic to chocolate or something?"

"My parents are dead. Have been for ten years."

"Ah. In that case . . ." Clare yanked his mattress off and slid under the bed, sheltering both of them behind the too-thin sheet of foam.

The guard gave a resonant burp, redolent of chocolate and—for some weird reason—peanut butter. Orange-white light poured from his open mouth. His eyes widened. Clare covered her head and jammed her fingers into her ears. A shockwave pounded through the floor and through her chest. Overhead, the steel bunkbed danced on bolted-down legs. Small chunks of carmine flesh spattered on walls, floor, and mattress. The stench of old meat and half-digested crap made her clap a hand over her nose.

"Holy . . ." She blinked at the mess. "Well, that was unexpected. It wasn't meant to explode. Not yet."

Time to go.

She squirmed from under the bed. Something gooey dripped onto her shoulder. More slid down the clear wall. "Ew. Revolting." The cell was now a vomit-inducing modern art piece any gallery would pay a fortune for.

MacDiarmid's fingers snagged her ankle again. Tighter, this time. "Get me out of here."

Clare considered the chaos. Outside, alarms wailed and lights flashed lockdown red. Other prisoners kicked at the clear alzin walls and rattled their doors, yelling obscenities—or cheering. Hard to tell. Distant booted footsteps thudded.

"What's in it for me?" She shook free of his clutch. After this, she certainly wasn't returning to MacDiarmid's not-parents.

He brought his other hand into view, complete with the ex-guard's muck-crusted disruptor. She froze.

MacDiarmid pointed the weapon at her.

And fired.

The disruptor field missed her by millimetres and something thumped to the floor behind her. Clare spun. A second Yasti guard—now more a blubbery, bloodied mess than a recognisable rodent—oozed to the ground. Clare's heart slid back down her throat and settled into its usual place in her chest. Her stomach tried to revolt. She swallowed.

"What's in it for you," Mac said through gritted teeth, "is the opportunity to live a few more years." He staggered, swaying, to his feet.

"I can just leave and have that," Clare shot back. "You're clearly trouble." She glanced at the dissolving guard. "Oh. And thanks."

"You're welcome. Thanks for the nose job," he replied. "Look, even if you get out of here alive, you'll need my help to stay that way."

"Why?"

"Because," he said, his gaze intense, "that cake wasn't meant for just me."

"What the . . . ?" she gaped, momentarily bereft of any witty comeback.

He waved the gun at the door. "Can we walk and talk at the same time?" He took a step but his leg folded and he grabbed at the bed. "Feckit! Maybe not."

"Cart?"

"Cart." He nodded. "I'll explain as we go. Name's Iain MacDiarmid."

"Too many vowels. If you want to get out of here, that will involve me yelling instructions, so you're Mac."

He sighed. "Fine."

She shoved the door open, stepped over soggy rat flesh, and swiped her wrist chip over the slightly-mangled lock. It beeped green.

Next, she helped Mac aboard and grabbed the cart handles. Unsurprisingly, one wheel showed an irritating tendency to wander in the wrong direction.

Along the hall, cell doors popped open.

"Your doing?" Mac jerked a thumb at the emerging prisoners.

"Could be just a terrible lockdown system." She ankle-tapped a guard as he ran at her. He tripped and audibly cracked his head on the cart. His eyes rolled back and he slumped.

Mac chuckled. "Or a virus you just slipped into their computers with your wrist chip? Pity you couldn't do that from the inside. Would have been less . . . messy."

"Not my fault your cake blew up the guard instead of the door."

He shot someone behind her and shrugged. "I'll give you that one."

"So?" she shouted over the noise of the rattling cart, sirens, screaming prisoners, and swearing guards.

Mac calmly shot another of the security staff, who slid messily down the wall. Clare drove around the body, trying not to puke. The cart's wheels smeared streaks of blood and brains behind her.

"I came here to hide," Mac called back. He hefted a small, heavy-looking package-scanner in one hand and hurled it at a leaping guard, knocking the man unconscious.

"From who?" Clare peeked around him and flicked her second dart at a prisoner wielding a broken off bed leg. He fell like an axed tree. She studied the hallway ahead. Right at the next junction should see them at the rear exit. Then it was just . . . well . . . a long run back to her safe little ship.

"The Chancer brothers," he replied. "That's who those 'parents' of mine probably were. Skinny blonde and a tall bald guy?"

"Yes. I *thought* they looked too young to be parents to a thirty-year-old. But you can never tell who's done youth re-gen these days. Wait!" Clare paused and he frowned at her. "Are you saying the Chancer brothers—whom no-one's ever met and who were a woman and a man, by the way—sent me here to help you escape?"

His grin turned feral, his eyes glittering in a way that indicated she should reconsider her agreement to help him escape. "Nope. I'm saying my half-brother and his wife—who are the third generation to bear the Chancer brothers name— sent you to find me. Then they sent the exploding cake to kill both of us."

"What the feck? Why?" A prisoner jumped at her and she jabbed her third dart into his arm. He keeled over, gargling.

Mac casually punched a guard unconscious then shook his hand and grimaced. "I'm guessing you owe them money?"

Clare nodded. "Duck, Mac!"

He dodged disruptor fire and gave her a nod. "You can kiss anything you own goodbye. They've stolen it by now."

"But I was going to pay them back!" she wailed. "This job would have paid me enough . . . oh, crap. Feckety feck feck feck!" She smacked her forehead. "Double-crossing . . ."

Mac's smile widened. "Yes. They do like to kill two birds. Or people, in this case. It's a trademark move. As is the exploding chocolate cake." He tilted his head and absently elbowed a guard in the throat. "Not sure why it's always chocolate to kill people."

"Because they're sadistic bastards," she muttered. "Chocolate should be sacrosanct." This was *not* turning out to be a good day. Having the Chancer brothers on her arse was going to make life difficult.

She turned the corner in a hurry to avoid a rabble of yelling prisoners. The cart tilted dangerously and Mac clung on, swearing at her bad driving.

The back exit lay only metres away.

Mac lifted his brows. "You do know this door is electronically sealed. Flashing red lights and all. Impossible to open unless you can kill the electronic lock *and* the manual one."

With a smirk, Clare rummaged in her underpants.

"Er . . ." Mac slid off the cart and edged away. "Flattering as this is, do you really think it's the right time and place?"

She produced the putty penis and he blanched. His mouth dropped open. One hand clutched his crotch.

"Relax. The name's Clare, by the way." She inspected her gnawed-off fingernails. Good. The three ceramic razorblades she'd had surgically implanted were still sharp. A few quick swipes turned the penis into diced pieces.

Mac whimpered.

A moment's work squashed the unattractive things between her palms, moulding them into skin-coloured lumps of sweaty-smelling putty.

Clare strolled to the door and slapped the putty over the electronic lock. She jammed in the detonator wire.

"Five seconds," she said, hiding behind the cart.

Mac collapsed beside her. This time the explosion was much smaller, more focussed. When it was done, the electronic lock was nothing but gently smoking wires and fused bits of metal. Clare picked the manual lock and eased the door open.

Behind her, Mac shot another guard and collected a second disruptor for his efforts.

"Right . . ." she whispered, surveying the dozen or so guards manning the fenced-in yard. "The *De Lune*'s not far. That's my flipship." She paused and reconsidered. "Well, when I say 'not far'—" she pointed west "—it's past the Grey Guards, across that wide-open kill-zone, over an electrified fence, past a kennel full of tracker-dogs, through a smallish jungle of poison-tipped sentient vines, and on the other side of a rather wide river. She's hidden in the crater of a somewhat dormant volcano."

He glanced at her quizzically. "Somewhat dormant?" She opened her mouth and he held up a hand. "Never mind. It's a terrible plan, anyway. How about we just take one of those hovers?" He pointed across the yard at the small, two-man, low altitude craft.

"Sure," Clare replied. "There's only an entire regiment of Grey Guards between it and us. What could go wrong? How do you propose to get to it?" She looked him over—bruised, bloodied, half-paralysed. "You're not in great condition."

Mac rose and managed a couple of steady steps. He bared straight white teeth. "I don't need to be. Does your ship have any black in it?"

"Always carry some. It's like universal criminal currency. Don't touch the shit myself."

"Well, it's been twelve hours since my last hit and the mail-delivery guard was my supplier." He hefted the two disruptors and chortled. "I'd like to see anyone stop me getting to it."

* * *

A short time later, Clare was still trying to shake the image of disruptor-shot Grey Guards dissolving into the black soil, when she thumbed open the latch on the *De Lune.* Nearby, lava burbled and plorped, hiding her ship from search parties with a cloud of steam and ash. The hover was now so much slag, melting in the bottom of the lava lake.

Mac hurried into the ship as soon as the door opened and rummaged through her medical cabinet. "Where's the black?"

Her final paralytic dart went into his neck. He spun, glaring, kept turning, swore, staggered, grabbed at the curved wall, missed, fell to his knees, swore again, and slumped on the floor.

Clare leaned closer. "Sorry, my friend, but if you're going to ride with me, you'll go cold turkey. Not that I don't trust you, you understand." She patted his head. "OK. I don't trust you."

His eyes rolled back.

* * *

Two days later, when she'd flipped the *De Lune* outside Hegemon-controlled space, Mac woke up complaining about the medi-bot attached to his arm. He rattled the straps holding him down.

"What the feck? Where are we?"

From her pilot's seat, Clare grinned over her shoulder at him. "You're not in Kansas, Toto."

"What does that even mean?"

"No clue. Something my grandmother used to say. It means we're a very long way from the Chancer brothers' very long reach. Needed to get your system blacked out. You're clean now. Better stay that way, too."

"Why?" he muttered. "The Hegemon is run by corrupt bureaucrats and policed by the equally-shitty Grey Guards. The Trader families control the trade run money. The crime syndicates—including my adorable family—run everything else. What's left to do? Prison was safer and black made a nice escape."

"Such pessimism!" Clare laughed. "What's left is for us to form our own crime syndicate. You can be the muscle. I can be the brains."

"That's not a syndicate. Not even a partnership. And I'm dubious about the "brains" bit." He eyed her narrowly. "But, just out of curiosity, what would our target market be?"

Clare swivelled her chair around and laced her hands behind her head. "We could work out near Catterman IV. People visiting pleasure planets were always so gullible and scams are *such* fun. Plus it will piss off the Chancer brothers. That's their territory."

He stilled, a slow smile spreading. "Hell, yes. I'm in."

She released the medi-bot and straps. He lurched to the front of the *De Lune* and fell into the co-pilot's seat.

"So, what'll we call this crime syndicate of ours? *Mac and Clare?*"

"Sounds too much like a terrible folk band. Or a hamburger. And your family knows my name." She tapped a finger to her lips and stared out at the stars. "I'd like to stay invisible. You can be the one people see."

"The one people can identify to assassins, you mean?"

"Maybe." Clare chuckled. "I know. *Mac and The Baggerman.*"

"What the feck is a baggerman?"

"No idea." She punched the co-ordinates for Catterman IV. "I'm making this up as I go along."

Mac sighed and scrubbed a hand over his face. "I can see I'm going to regret this, aren't I?"

"Probably."

About the Author:

Aiki Flinthart has 13 published novels and two non-fiction books, along with numerous short stories published in various anthologies and e-magazines.

Her stories have been shortlisted in the Australian Aurealis Awards and she has been twice a top-8 finalist in the USA Writers of the Future competition.

When not writing, Aiki likes to practice fantasy-approved hobbies such as martial arts, archery, knife-throwing, lute-playing, and belly-dancing.

You can find her at www.aikiflinthart.com, or on Facebook, Twitter, and Instagram—she's the only Aiki Flinthart.

ABOUT MELANOMA INSTITUTE
AUSTRALIA

Melanoma Institute Australia (MIA) pioneers advances in melanoma research and treatment that are making a difference to the lives of patients today.

We are a non-profit organisation dedicated to preventing and curing melanoma through innovative, world-class research, treatment and education programs.

MIA is a national affiliated network of melanoma researchers and clinicians based in Sydney at the Poche Centre – the world's largest melanoma research and treatment facility. It's from here that our specialists pioneer new research, conduct clinical trials, develop new treatments and promote awareness of melanoma and where our clinics treat 1,500 melanoma patients each year.

www.melanoma.org.au/

Supporting

ABOUT DEADSET PRESS

Deadset Press is an independent publisher of incredible speculative fiction. We provide publishing pathways for emerging writers from Australia and New Zealand, and aspire to shine the light on unique and diverse voices. You can learn more at:

www.deadsetpress.com

ALSO BY DEADSET PRESS